"Scofield does not pull her punches. . . . At the core of this novel is a deep-rooted belief in the nurturing ethos."
—*New York Times Book Review*

"A rich tapestry of two women's lives . . . We come to understand the kinds of richness—and sacrifice—Dulce and Maggie will bring to their new families, and we, too, are enriched."
—*Dallas Morning News*

"Scofield offers trenchant but understated studies of human relationships that touch the heart as well as the intellect. . . . A rare and moving combination of love, strength and humor."
—*Publishers Weekly*

"Moves gracefully between the loosely connected worlds of self and family . . . Genuine . . . Gut-honest."
—*Detroit Free Press*

SANDRA SCOFIELD is the author of the novels *Beyond Deserving*, which was nominated for a National Book Award and won an American Book Award, *Walking Dunes*, and the forthcoming *Gringa* (all Plume), as well as *Opal on Dry Ground*. She lives in Ashland, Oregon.

MORE THAN ALLIES

SANDRA SCOFIELD

A PLUME BOOK

PLUME
Published by the Penguin Group
Penguin Books USA Inc., 375 Hudson Street,
New York, New York 10014, U.S.A.
Penguin Books Ltd, 27 Wrights Lane, London W8 5TZ, England
Penguin Books Australia Ltd, Ringwood, Victoria, Australia
Penguin Books Canada Ltd, 10 Alcorn Avenue,
Toronto, Ontario, Canada M4V 3B2
Penguin Books (N.Z.) Ltd, 182–190 Wairau Road, Auckland 10, New Zealand

Penguin Books Ltd, Registered Offices:
Harmondsworth, Middlesex, England

Published by Plume, an imprint of Dutton Signet, a division of
Penguin Books USA Inc. This is an authorized reprint of a hardcover edition
published by The Permanent Press. For information address
The Permanent Press, Noyac Road, Sag Harbor, NY 11963.

First Plume Printing, November, 1994
10 9 8 7 6 5 4 3 2 1

LIBRARY OF CONGRESS CATALOGING-IN-PUBLICATION DATA
Scofield, Sandra Jean.
More than allies : a novel / by Sandra Scofield.
p. cm.
ISBN 0-452-27306-4
1. Friendship—Fiction. 2. Women—Fiction. 3. Oregon—Fiction.
I. Title.
PS3569.C584M67 1994
813'.54—dc20 94–17417
CIP

Printed in the United States of America

PUBLISHER'S NOTE
This is a work of fiction. Names, characters, places, and incidents either are the product of the author's imagination or are used fictitiously, and any resemblance to actual persons, living or dead, events, or locales is entirely coincidental.

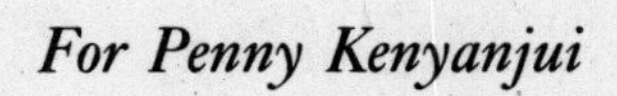

For Penny Kenyanjui

Acknowledgements:

* * *

I would like to thank Joan Kalvelage, Jane Barry, Patty Wixon, and Tod Davies for their essential insights; Judy Shepard for her apt and delicate editorial hand; Bonnie Comfort and Jan Gregory for all the phone calls; and Kre Kalvelage, Penny Colvin, Janice Gabriel, Leah Ireland, Barbara Davidson, Jan Mahoney, and Nancy Peterson for information and ideas I used in my own arbitrary ways.

S.S.

Woman is woman's natural ally.

—EURIPIDES

MORE THAN ALLIES

June 1992

* * *

South of Lupine, the highway ascended rapidly, curving in broad swaths along the rim of the valley. It was early, and the mountains, in shadows, looked a cool blue. At the top, they were ribbed with pink morning light. We pulled off at the turnout. There were several other cars parked, people out for a better look. A couple held an elderly woman between them by her elbows, as if she might beat her arms and fly away. A woman in a long green sweater sat on a rock, smoking, while a man stood beside her, talking without looking at her.

We watched the boys, like puppies, taking the air. They pummeled one another, then climbed a flat boulder and waved to us. They made faces and posed, though nobody had a camera.

It's going to be a long drive, I told her. I wish we had some of those books on tape. Not that I have a player. I don't even have a radio.

She said: We can talk.

I did have things I wanted to talk about. I had things to figure out. There would be time. Sure, I said.

You can tell me about your friends.

But you already know them!

I don't think we know the same things, she said. They never talked to me.

I guess they wouldn't, I said, then I glanced over to see if I'd offended her. She didn't seem to notice. I wanted to tell her, my friends didn't listen.

We can talk about our children, she said. It did seem odd, that the boys knew each other so much better than we women did.

We should have done that sooner.

And our husbands, she said.

I was surprised; she seemed so private. I thought I would like to know what she thought about love, and if I, in turn, spoke my own feelings—we had no history, she and I—I might hear what I really thought.

Really, it's ourselves, I said. We should talk about ourselves.

I might not be good at that.

I told her: We have lots of time.

Be patient, she said. This is new for me. I never belonged to a group, like you. I'm not used to talking.

By then we were over the pass into California. On that side, the hills looked like camel-brown suede. I told her: Go ahead. You start.

I wanted her to tell me how to be strong like her. She had been alone a long time. I wanted to say, tell me how to be still, how not to cry. I always thought other people knew things I did not. I always wondered how they had learned earlier, and more easily.

She said she dreamed, and she wrote her dreams in a notebook. She said: I dreamed about you. Last night. I saw you in a house, on the second floor. I saw you from across a large yard. You were standing at a window. I don't know what you were doing, but I thought you were smiling.

What a nice dream. I hardly ever dream.

Everybody dreams. You have to tell yourself to remember. You have to tell yourself it's better to know.

Mmm, I murmured. I had found that when people didn't speak, it was usually because they knew they could hurt you. Dreams might be like that, or the mind's openness to dreams. I knew I would never invite dreams, or write them down. And even if it is true that everybody has dreams, I might never know what mine were. I thought for me that was best.

February 1979

* * *

She was worrying about her report on angels. She had been working on it over a month. She had a lot of notes. What would they be good for now? She might have made an A; her English grade was important to her. At first her teacher had tried to talk her out of the subject; she had a policy not to allow religious topics. I'm not religious, she argued. I don't even know if I believe in God. But angels—I think I saw one once.

The teacher said, let's separate that from the report. You can write about the angel you saw in your journal, for a free-writing assignment, if you want. For the report, though, think about angels across time, across cultures—an angel survey. See what people have thought about them. See what you can learn about early representations of angels. Did the ancient Greeks have angels? Did the Egyptians? What do Hindus believe? Moslems? Jews?

Of course you can write about angels! the teacher said. They've fascinated people throughout all ages. It was almost as if she were trying to talk her into the topic, when she'd started out trying to talk her out of it.

"I bet we'll come up out of this fog in a minute," the social worker, Mrs. Lyons, was saying. The sky had been gray and damp and cold for a couple of days now. You couldn't see the hills. "I could use a little sunshine," she added, as if she had problems made worse by the lack of light.

All the things Maggie had read about angels mentioned light, and sometimes fire. She'd thought of angels as sweet and beautiful, until she began reading about them. They could be majestic, even fierce. Some people believed in demons—fallen angels, as terrible as they had once been wonderful.

Mrs. Lyons took the first Lupine exit. They drove past some houses, and then, as she predicted, the sky cleared. They stopped at a light by a school. Little kids in fat jackets scurried across the street under the eye of the crosswalk guard. For the next few blocks, they passed big old houses on lots high above the sidewalks, and then they were in town, driving by shops. "You'll see the most wonderful gardens here in spring," Mrs. Lyons said. "Not just beds, but sometimes whole lots, filled with color. I drive over just to see them.

"The Jarretts live at the other end," she continued, "but I thought you'd like going through town and seeing what it looks like. You've never been over here, isn't that right?"

Maggie's cheeks burned. She felt stupid. She'd grown up at the other end of the valley, twenty-five miles away, and for the past year she'd been living closer in than that, but she'd never been anywhere. If you were a debater or an athlete, you had a reason to go to Lupine—there was a college there—or if you went on one of the school Shakespeare Theatre visits—but she had never been in extracurricular activities, and she had never signed up to go to a play.

"You're very lucky with this placement," Mrs. Lyons went on. "The Jarretts haven't taken a child in years. They're wonderful people. He's the fire chief."

"Oh," she said, because she didn't want Mrs. Lyons to think she was pouting, but what difference did it make to her what Mr. Jarrett did for a living? How lucky was she supposed to feel? All she cared was that they did not, like the last family, have horses. There had been terrible quarrels because she did not want to clean out stalls or feed the animals. She was willing to wash dishes, do laundry, sweep and mop. She didn't complain about watching the younger children, though they were dull and bratty. But she didn't think it was up to her to take care of animals. They weren't hers. Finally, she had simply refused to come out of her room. The woman had argued and argued, and then had shaken her. When Mrs. Lyons came, the woman said Maggie provoked her. It wasn't like she struck her. She wasn't a baby, with an unformed brain.

"The daughter is a sophomore, too," Mrs. Lyons said. "I'm sure you'll be friends."

Maggie nodded. It took great effort, as if her head were held down by lead weights. She didn't understand why she was being moved to another town. She had talked to a girl in her geometry class who was going to ask her parents if she could stay with them. She'd just needed a little more time. It didn't seem fair that she should change schools now, when she was ready to write her report. She hadn't had any warning, hadn't had time to ask the teacher if she would be credited in her transfer grade with the effort she had made. Maybe the Lupine class would be doing reports, now or later, and she could write up what she'd learned about angels then. Assuming she had a new teacher who could be enthusiastic because she was, who would be willing to allow angels as a topic even if religion had no place in school.

The Jarretts lived on a quiet street with no sidewalks, almost out of town. Their house was the deep shiny red of nail polish, with white trim. It looked out across the tops of houses at hills dusted with snow. Mrs. Jarrett met them in the drive, reaching out for Maggie's things. All she had was a suitcase and a backpack. "Come in, come in!" Mrs. Jarrett said, the way you would think she would greet relatives.

She took her down a short hallway. "This will be your room," she said. "The bath is right across the hall, you share that with Gretchen. We're in the corner over there." She patted a cupboard door in the hall. "Towels, help yourself. There's a laundry basket in the bathroom." Maggie was clutching her backpack against her chest. "Oh goodness," Mrs. Jarrett said, "I'm telling you a lot more than you need to know. Why don't you set your things down, and then come into the kitchen? I'll get us something to drink."

Maggie heard their voices, low, concerned, friendly, while she looked around the room. Everything that would have made the room *somebody's* was gone. She could see where there had been posters on the wall. There were shelves, now empty. The spread on the bed, a pretty pink print, was obviously new. She sat down on the edge and pressed hard into the center of the bed. It seemed okay. It didn't have any big depressions from whoever had been sleeping in it. Butt-rutts, she called them. They made her feel intrusive; they were too intimate.

Suddenly she was so sleepy she wanted nothing so much as to lie face forward on the new pink spread and sleep until morning, when she would go to school, but she looked up and saw Mrs. Lyons in the doorway, smiling at her in a way that said, let's get off on the right foot here.

She followed her back to the kitchen, and sat at the table across from Mrs. Jarrett, who offered her cookies from a plate, and a cup of tea. Maggie declined a cookie; they weren't homemade, so she didn't think it would hurt Mrs. Jarrett's feelings. She stared into her cup. The tea had almost no color, and a funny odor. She took a sip, and gasped. Both women stared.

"It's hot," she said. The smell made her think of the hay they fed horses.

Mrs. Jarrett's hand went to her mouth. "Oh, I've given you herb tea and you don't like it."

"It's all right," she said meekly.

"Of course it's not," Mrs. Jarrett said, clearing the cup away quickly. "I'm sorry."

Tears sprang to Maggie's eyes. There was no way she was going to be able to answer questions. She couldn't be interesting and grateful and polite all at once, if ever, and certainly not right now, when she was too sleepy to speak at all.

Mrs. Jarrett handed her a bottle of Coke and a napkin. "You can take this down to your room, if you like, dear," she said. "I bet you're not the least bit interested in sitting here with us right this minute." She patted Maggie's hand. "We're going to have a long time to get to know one another. I bet you'd rather be by yourself a little while."

Both grateful and embarrassed, Maggie fled without telling Mrs. Lyons goodbye. She drank some of the Coke and set it on the table by the bed, then opened her suitcase. Her belongings had been hastily packed; her blouses were wrinkled. Some of the clothes were dirty. She picked up a skirt she liked, a simple flared corduroy she had made in Home Ec in the fall. She rubbed the nap, the way she had rubbed a stuffed pig she'd had as a child. She had no idea what had happened to that pig. She wished she still had it.

She thought Mrs. Jarrett was nice. She thought things would be okay in this red house. She would get used to another school.

There were two pillows on the bed. She smacked them. One was hard, one soft. She kicked off her shoes and crawled onto the spread, covering her arms with her jacket. She lay on the hard pillow, and covered her head with the soft one.

When she woke, it was dark. She could hear a television, the sound of voices, and kitchen noises. She smelled food, and she realized she was hungry.

She went across the hall to the bathroom and washed. As she stepped out, she saw a girl in the doorway of her room. The girl turned. She looked so much like Maggie, in size and coloring, her hair long and limp on her shoulders, there was an instant of recognition for both of them.

"I came to tell you supper's ready," the girl said. "I'm Gretchen. You're Margaret?"

"Maggie." She reached back to turn off the bathroom light.

"We're having chicken. Mother's a good cook."

They both stepped into the hall. Maggie looked over Gretchen's shoulder. "Was that a boy's room?" she asked. Gretchen said it was.

"He didn't die, did he?" Maggie said. She didn't think she could sleep in the room of someone who had died.

Gretchen laughed. "He just went to the army," she said. "He left the day after Christmas."

It was a terrible thing to have said. "Don't tell your mother I asked that," Maggie said.

Gretchen took hold of Maggie's elbow. "Don't worry about Mother," she said. "Don't worry about anything. Really, that room is your room now. You're home, Maggie. Mother says an angel sent you. She can't stand an empty bed. She needs you. You'll see. She's got to have people to look out for. She's got too much energy for just Dad and me. You've come to the right place. I don't know what you've been through, why you don't have your own family to be with, but I promise, you'll be happy here. Don't tell Mom I made a big deal out of it. But don't worry anymore. You'll be happy."

May 1992

* * *

Maggie heard the baby crying, but tunneled deeply into sleep, she thought it was from far away. A neighbor baby. She woke when Jay stood by her bed, shaking her shoulder . "I think Stevie's sick," he said. With no more light than the night light by the crib, she could see that his Garfield shirt had a big stain on it. Grape juice, his current passion.

"I'm sorry, honey," she told him. She squeezed his elbow. "Go back to bed." He slept on a day bed in the living room of the little cottage. Stevie slept in an alcove made out of what had been the closet. Maggie sat up and rubbed her eyes. Stevie barked once, that awful croupy cough she'd had before, and then she made a soft, mewling sound. Jay stumbled off to bed.

As Maggie picked her up, Stevie tried to cry louder, but only a pitiful thin whimper came out. She was hot, her pajama top damp with perspiration. Maggie held her and walked over to switch on the lamp on the dresser. The way Stevie looked frightened her. She was pale and damp, and her lips were dark. She was gasping, sucking in air, her little chest heaving. Maggie felt her forehead and called Jay.

"Run in and tell Granny I need her, honey. Tell her to bring a thermometer."

Her son groaned. Maggie reached out to touch him on the shoulder. "Then go to bed in the house, we'll be up out here. Thank you. I don't know what I'd do without you, Jay-Jay." As he headed out, his T-shirt billowed in the back, and Maggie could see his underpants drooping in the seat.

Polly didn't think they should fool around. She held the baby while Maggie dressed, then ran back in to dress herself. On the way to the hospital, Maggie said, "I can't let you pay for this. What'll they say? With no insurance?"

Polly said not to worry. The hospital had a sign up in the emergency room: We Serve Our Community. "I'll talk to them about it," she offered. "They'll charge you something less, and Mo will send money. All that matters right now is to see to Stevie."

The baby felt so warm against Maggie's chest, steam seemed to rise. "Shh, shh," she soothed, though the baby was barely whimpering. Every once in a while she'd suck in air, then bark, then subside again to her pitiful sounds. "I'm scared," Maggie said, but by then they were there.

They thought maybe the baby had swallowed something that was stuck in her windpipe, or even in a lung. Maggie couldn't think what that would be. They handled the baby all over, less gently than Maggie thought they should, but maybe it was the haste, the need, that made them seem rough. They said they had to take an X-ray, they didn't know what they were looking for. One of the nurses led her back into the sitting room, where she huddled against Polly.

Polly put her arm around her. She stroked her hair and shushed and whispered. Maggie felt like the child. She needed to feel that way; it was too overwhelming to see her own child struggling to breathe. Jay had never scared her like this. He had had all the things babies have: colds and diarrhea, earaches and rashes. He had been a screamer, too, yowling when a diaper rubbed him the wrong way or he was hungry, but Mo had loved that, loved to say, Listen to that kid, won't you! Stevie was different, not fragile or sickly, but quiet and watchful and almost sad. Maggie thought it was because Mo left when he did, just when Stevie started to walk. She liked to toddle back and forth across the room, but she had to go between Maggie and a chair. Her daddy was gone.

The ER doctor came out and sat in a chair across from Maggie and Polly. Maggie's heart threatened to thud out of her chest. He smiled, though. He said whatever it was appeared to be over. "Baby is breathing freely," he said. They thought that a cold virus had come on so suddenly and fiercely, Baby had coughed up a knot of phlegm and it had plugged her throat, like a chunk of carrot or a quarter, cutting off her airway. With all the handling, and her attempts to cry, the phlegm had finally been freed and spit up. "She's really quite all right," he said. "You can take her home." He had more to say—not to give her aspirin for the fever, to give her plenty of water—but Maggie couldn't concentrate. She didn't have to. She knew Polly would know what to do.

At home, they laid Stevie in the crib at the end of

the hallway, against the linen closet, between the doors to Polly's and Gretchen's rooms. Polly said she thought they could use a cup of cocoa.

They sat companionably at the polished round table, both of them facing the windows so they could look at the hills and watch morning come on. Maggie said, "I don't know what I'd do without you." She couldn't believe all the years that had gone by. She still felt, often, like a child, though she was twenty-eight and twice a mother herself.

Polly said, "You're stronger than you know, dear." She got up and pulled out canisters and bowls and the beaters. "I might as well make something hot for breakfast," she said. "Jay-Jay likes muffins so much."

Maggie watched her work, enjoying the rhythm of her movements, the crack of the eggs, the whirr of the beaters, the sound of the spatula scraping the sides of the bowl. Polly put two pans in the oven, then turned and leaned back against the counter.

"I'm going to have a foster baby soon," she said. "Maybe by the end of the week."

Maggie felt as if Polly had smacked her. Polly helped with the children—did as much as Maggie, really—and was a respite caretaker for a hospice. She was on committees at the Grange and church. Why did she need a baby?

Polly's fist pressed against her breast. "It's like a little cry that tugs at me right here, babies being born these days to mothers who can't take care of them. Babies sick before they're even born." She smiled. "It's vain of me, isn't it? To think they need me? To think I could do something important, taking care of one of them."

Maggie glanced at the clock by the oven. It was

almost seven. "I'm supposed to sub this afternoon. The teacher's going to a drug conference." She yawned.

"Maybe you should call in," Polly suggested.

"I don't think they want to get subs for their subs," Maggie said. "Maybe if I got a little nap."

"I can get Jay off to school," Polly said. She didn't look nearly as tired as Maggie felt. "And Gretchen will be up after a while. She can watch Stevie while I sleep."

"That's great, about the baby," Maggie said. "Lucky baby."

"Maybe Stevie will be pleased, too," Polly said. "Maybe she'll feel big with an infant in the house."

Maggie gave Polly a hug. "Sorry about last night. The false alarm. I really was scared."

"Why, so was I! There are no false alarms with children. Worry is always real."

Maggie nodded, and left. She thought she was just beginning to understand what Polly meant. Worry seemed to be the main verb in Maggie's life these days. She worried about her children, about money, about her moribund marriage, she even worried about politics. She would be depending on Polly until one of them was dead.

* * *

San Marcos, Texas

Querida,

You haven't written to say if the money I sent you arrived, and whether you will come here, at least to visit, as my mama has written so many times to beg you, and now I too plead. It was a wonderful feeling to write out a money order to you, out of the very first money I earned since I was released. I am working with mi hermano Ricky, making the wheels of asadero cheese I missed so much these past years.

You don't know what I have suffered, I don't want you to know, and I promise not to talk about it to you or Gus, except to answer questions if they come up, because I don't want to pretend something didn't happen when it did. My son will soon be a man. Don't you think I could grow up, too? I know I wasn't good to you, and I know I was an idiot, a true fool not to be serious and not to be afraid enough of the consequences of temper and bad luck and bad judgment, but if I did or did not deserve what I got (and I think I didn't, but it is a waste to be bitter), still I chose right, to become a better person and a better chicano, instead of a hard man. I am strong now, inside and out, although my mama likes to fuss over me like I only left last year when I was fifteen, and I am smarter, too, because I know to pay atten-

tion, and besides, didn't I do a year of college courses to have something to show for all the time?

I understand why you have drawn around you a shawl of silence and privacy, and I do not criticize you, but I ask, how is your attitude—that you must fit in, although only on the edges—any less fatalistic than the poorest indio's? If you do not yearn, and reach. If you do not believe you are in control of your life, if you do not think you can see Gus grow strong and well and happy, with some fair share of bounty, then you, who has cut herself off from her own people, are the oppressed peasant.

It is beautiful here. What a fool I was, a crazy boy, to leave it, but if I had not, I would never have known you, I would never have had Gus, life has its way. But I see now how lucky I am, because my family has made a good life here. There is hope here. Land for the family, independent and good work, neighbors and friends, and oh, the cows and goats and chickens. You and I should be together. There is a reason you have never divorced, and now you must think what the reason is. Maybe it is only Gus, and not love, but Gus is a reason. Maybe all I can hope for is to be with him, and maybe only time to time, but I tell you what I want, to be a family. Not overnight, but in time.

I ask you with humility and love, be open. See for yourself and do not feel pushed. Se lo pido de corazón: perdón.

Recibe un abrazo y muchos besos para ti y mi hijo—

Gustavo

p.s. Send photos

Dulce pulled the heavy spread off the bed and piled it on a chair, then began stripping off the linens. You could go for weeks, every room perfectly routine, and then there would be one like this. Right in the cleft between the pillows was a used condom. One of the pillowcases was stained—a bloody nose?—and all the trash in the room—papers, magazines, cups, disposable razors, tissues, bottles and cans—was on the floor. The trash baskets were pristine. The towels were on the bathroom and dressing room floors, sopping, and the corner of the bathroom mirror had a lipstick drawing of what Dulce assumed was meant to be a penis. They had had a good time. Lovers, you supposed. Married people didn't act like this.

By noon she had done the nine rooms assigned her. The housekeeper told her they would be able to put her on a five-day schedule in June, for the summer. She would earn some sick time, some vacation time, too; they let her carry the sick days season to season, while they laid her off during the winter, and she always took the vacation pay at Christmas. She said that would be fine. She didn't know how to be enthusiastic; the housekeeper didn't expect it, anyway. They knew she'd show up every morning, she'd do the work, she'd never complain. She was surprised to hear they would give her a thirty-cent an hour raise in June, too. She had worked for the motel three years; this was her second raise.

She drove home slowly, uneasy about the car, which had been overheating the last few days if she went above twenty miles an hour. At home, she ate a cheese sandwich, then showered and changed into a skirt and sweater. She walked over to the grade school. Her son Gus was in fourth grade, in the "tri-level classroom," a melange of children from grades three through five. The principal had recommended the placement last year, because there was so much range in Gus' skills—he was a whiz in math, a little behind in reading, and practically illiterate in his writing. She explained that there would be a lot more flexibility in Gus' grouping for instruction, and less pressure or possible embarrassment about working in skill groups "perceived to be below grade level." Dulce thought a little pressure might be exactly what Gus required, but she always lost her tongue at school, even though everybody there was as nice as they could be. Besides, she assumed they knew more about teaching than she did, though she hoped she knew Gus best. The teacher, Jack, said she shouldn't worry. He thought Gus would read and write just fine when he was ready. He was nine years old; how ready would he have to be? Sometimes she thought she ought to take away his colored pencils and pens; he drew endlessly, and read comic books, though with better weather, and his friendship with Hilario, he was outdoors a lot more than he used to be.

She went into the school through the cafeteria, then cut over to let the office know she was in the building.

As soon as the secretary saw her, she smiled and gave her a wave. Parents with children in the "Tri-L's" were expected to put in time in their children's classrooms. Most wanted to know everything that was happening; she was always getting notes and flyers about projects and concerns. Should the children raise money for a garden or send cash to Somalia? Who would go on the camping trip to the Redwoods with them, and who had tents? Was Jack stepping over some boundary when he had them do visualization exercises before creative writing? Should the children be allowed to bring candy in their brown bag lunches? And why were they required to take standardized tests like the regular classroom students?

At the classroom door, she scanned the room, looking for the teacher, and for her son. Jack was under the loft with a couple of kids, his head bent over their work, his hair sweeping his cheek. He was totally absorbed, though the room was swarming with activity. That was the first thing she had noticed about him, his ability to attend wholly to a child or a group. Above him, on the loft, which was piled with huge pillows, two boys were wrestling while a girl lay stretched out on her stomach, reading. At the table in the corner, a mother was sewing something; the old machine whirred and clacked, and two little girls hovered over her, chattering and bouncing. A boy was cleaning out the gerbil cage; the trash can by him was overflowing, and spilling onto the floor. Nowhere was anyone seated at a desk; in fact, there were no desks in the room, only tables, but no one was seated there, either. A couple of kids lay flat on their backs on a rug, holding books up over their heads. There was no sign of Gus.

A tiny girl—could she really be a third grader?—

came up and took Dulce's arm. "Lechuga," she said. "Qué bonita." Obviously, the eager child, with her tiny Spanish vocabulary, knew whose mother Dulce was. Dulce knelt down beside her and said hello. In slow careful Spanish, she asked her name. The little girl's eyes squinched with effort, and finally she blurted out her age, "siete." She threw herself against Dulce and hugged her. Dulce gave her a squeeze, and stood up.

"Do you know where Gus is?" she asked.

"In the gym. They're practicing for Spanish night."

"Ahh," Dulce said. She knew what she was here for, then. Jack had asked her in September if she would tutor the kids in Spanish, but she declined. She wasn't a teacher; she didn't even have a high school diploma. At that time there was no one to whom she even spoke Spanish; only since Hilario's family came to town had she any call for it. So she had shown up a couple of times a month and listened to children read, or helped with crafts projects. In the beginning, Gus had stayed near her, but in the last couple of months he had made sure he had something to do unrelated to her. She noticed that most kids were like that when their parents came.

She walked slowly to the gym. Along the hallway she looked at children's drawings posted on the walls. Outside one classroom was a long stretch of butcher paper on which the kids had drawn an underwater scene: fish and odd, unidentifiable creatures, plants with wavy tendril arms. The next stretch of drawings were copies of famous paintings; she recognized Van Gogh's sunflowers, and the Midwestern farm couple with the rake and stern faces.

In the gym she saw Gus right away. He and Hilario

and a third student were working with a video camera in the back of the room. She saw him see her, and she smiled and waved. He nodded. His hands were busy with the camera.

At the front, on the stage, some kids were practicing their skit in front of a makeshift set constructed from a refrigerator carton. One child was wearing a cape, and another had a frilly hat on his head. She approached them, and Jay, with whom Gus used to spend most his time, called out, "Oh good, it's Dulce!" which made her relax and remember she was the adult and these were children.

They were practicing the story of Little Red Riding Hood. "Qué dientes tan grandes tienes!" they recited. She listened to the skit all the way through, slightly amused. They had been working on Spanish all year with one of the fathers, a pharmacist who went somewhere in Central America every winter for a while. Also, there was a teacher who came in once a week to drill the kids on vocabulary; Gus liked to recite the names of fruits and vegetables, and would sometimes blurt out, "Hace sol hoy," or the like.

The students hit the sounds of "d" and "t" too hard, and they wandered in and out of the proper ending on the word for grandparent, but Dulce couldn't imagine that anyone would care or even notice except her and the Spanish teacher, who couldn't be everywhere at once. Dulce praised the kids and went through the skit again. She suggested that they speak a little louder. Their parents would want to hear everything. They said they needed to work on the set. They were drawing the grandmother's window on the cardboard. Dulce went to see what her son was doing.

The kids were taping family stories. Hilario had

first told his in Spanish, then, with help, had written an English version and memorized it. "You like to hear?" Hilario asked now. Dulce agreed she would. They couldn't play the tape—there was no TV set up in the gym—but Hilario was eager to do his recitation. She sank to the floor, and some of the kids from the stage sat down around her, while others wandered off, back to the classroom.

Hilario stood up straight. He was a full head taller than the next tallest child in the class. He should have been in sixth or seventh grade, but with his poor English and lack of school experience, the middle school counselor had sent him over to the Tri-L class, where he would have fewer demands and a relaxed structure. It was true that he had learned a lot since his February arrival, but Dulce couldn't help wondering where they would put him next year, and just how far behind he really was. She would have thought he would work twice as hard to catch up, but he was enjoying being King Cock in grade school. For all practical purposes, Gus had a crush on him.

Jay, who had been one of the chorus reciting the wolf's lines in the skit, settled down close to Dulce. She reached out and put her arm on his shoulder. He moved in even more.

Hilario said, in his broken English, but rather better than Dulce would have thought he could, that his story was about something that happened to his mother when she was a little girl. She and her sister had gone to feed the pigs inside a fenced area. Her sister fell off the fence and into the mud with the pigs. She screamed, and when she jumped back up, she had pulled her hand inside the sleeve of her blouse, so that Hilario's mother, Lupe, could not see it. Lupe thought that a pig had bitten off her sister's hand, and she ran back to their mother shouting, "The pig ate her hand!"

The kids who had gathered around for Hilario's telling clapped, somebody whistled. Hilario beamed. Jay had disappeared.

A bell rang. It was time for recess. Dulce told Hilario she liked his story. She asked about his family. He went back to Spanish. His father was still in Mexico, where he had gone because his mother was sick. They had received a letter.

He looked through the windows at the torrent of children pouring onto the playground. "Go play," Dulce told him in English. She looked around, but Gus was gone.

Then she realized there was a commotion in the front of the gym. She ran back up to the stage to find that the "set" had been knocked down and trampled, and that several boys were scuffling. She ran around to go on the stairs up to the stage. She could hear someone screaming. It turned out to be Jay. It took several moments to figure out what had happened. He had found a can of red spray paint on a shelf at the back of the stage, and had sprayed it on the back of the set. When another boy saw the paint, he lunged for it and Jay sprayed his shirt. Now there was paint on the floor, too, and in the scuffle Jay had hurt his cheek. Kids wandering through the gym clustered at the foot of the stage to see what was going on. Some of them were giggling. She heard one of the older boys in Gus' room tell Jay, "You're going to get it!"

She didn't know what she was supposed to do. She was afraid she would be blamed—rightly, perhaps, but what could she have done? She couldn't be in two parts of the large room at the same time.

A girl came up and told her there shouldn't have been the paint on the stage. Very primly she informed her, "Dangerous things are supposed to be locked up." Dulce, recognizing budding authority, asked the little girl if she would go get the kids' teacher. He was there in two minutes. He apologized to Dulce. He said he hadn't realized that many children were out of the room. He studied the paint on the stage floor; it looked like red dust. He seemed quite anxious about it. Glancing over sternly at the kids, now lined up mutely along the stage front, seated with their legs dangling over the edge, he said, "You shouldn't have to worry about behavior when you come." Dulce wondered what he would say to Jay, but when she glanced down the row of youngsters, she didn't see him there at all. As she left the room, she heard the others shouting their explanations; Jay's name rang out like a bell, over and over. Jay did it. It was Jay's fault. What are you going to do to Jay?

She stopped in the girls' bathroom. Little girls were shuffling and yelling. She thought she saw feet under all the stalls. She waited a moment for one to open, then went in. In the toilet was one of the longest turds she had ever seen in her life. She stepped right back out, and saw the girl who had come out of that stall, and before she had thought about it, she reached out and grabbed her arm.

The child looked up in astonishment, and several other girls around her stared, suddenly quiet. Dulce felt her temples pounding, but stumbled on. She pulled the girl over and pointed at the toilet bowl. "You left it nasty! If you don't flush that, who do you think will?" The girl was wide-eyed and quiet. The other girls giggled. Dulce let go, embarrassed at her outburst, and the girl rushed over to flush the toilet, then ran out, followed by her friends, now jabbering shrilly.

Dulce leaned back against the wooden door of the stall. She had an insane urge to giggle. She couldn't think what had gotten into her. Maybe when you have scrubbed out as many toilets as she had, you lose patience with carelessness. Maybe she was getting old and minding too much business.

Maybe God was working hard to make her glad she wasn't a teacher!

* * *

Austin, Texas

Dear Maggie,

This isn't a good way for us to live. We have to decide whether we will be a family. I want that, but I don't believe we can make it, there. I need work, and you want work, and our children need both parents. I'm not going to say things over again about Mother, I know I said them too baldly when I left. I love her, and I know you do, too, but you are the mother now.

Austin is very beautiful, not like Lupine, but not completely unlike Lupine, either, because it is green and hilly. The main thing is, it's bigger, and I can make a living here. Maybe we won't be rich, but we could rent a house here, we could do that. They tell me the schools are okay. The music is everywhere, and great. They have nice little places to go and drink beer, they call them beer gardens, like in Germany. And lots of cheap places to eat.

If you would come down, and try it, see how you feel, I would stay open to living somewhere else, if there's work, but not Lupine. I am living in a one-room apartment in a house chopped up into apartments, but if you come I will rent a little house for the summer. It's hot here already, but there's water, many places to swim, good hamburgers. Jerry's wife is nice and wants to meet you. They have a baby a little older than Stevie. (They guessed which musician she was named for, which shows you they knew me pretty good right away!)

I thought you could come when school is out, since you won't be subbing. If you don't want to come, I want Jay for the summer. He can stay with me at the shop, or at Jerry's some of the time. I want to find an old car and start showing him how to work on engines. I promise I won't let him on a motorcycle, I know how you feel about that.

If you aren't going to come, we need to come to an agreement about child support and stuff, and whether you want a divorce, oh Maggie, not that! But I don't feel right sending you what I decide, I don't know what I ought to be doing, but I can tell you the only reason I haven't sent more is because I was saving up for security deposits for renting a house and turning on the utilities, and I overhauled the engine on the truck.

Well, school will be out pretty soon and there's no real reason for you not to come. I promise you you won't be nearly as lonesome as you think you will. Jerry's wife (Lisa) is dying for you to come, and I've already got to know some other people, too. You'd meet people because of the kids, especially when they're in school. What else can I say? I didn't say I love you, I miss you all the time, I've been true to you but I don't like being alone at all. If you want I will come get you, or we can use some of what I've saved and you can fly, except that you couldn't bring very much stuff.

Maybe you could talk to Mom about it. Not your friends. I don't mean don't talk to them, God don't get mad like I've insulted them or something. I just mean they're not the best ones to understand us. They're not really like us. Mom wants us together. I bet she prays for it, if I know her. There's a Mexican works in the shop, he says everything that happens, his wife goes to church and lights candles. If I was Catholic, that's what I'd do. I'd light all the candles in the place, and every one, I'd say, please let Maggie and the kids come. Please let me say the right things instead of the wrong things this time.

Love, Mo

Mrs. Tobler's English class had just finished reading *Death of a Salesman*. She had left a list of discussion questions. Maggie looked over the afternoon's plans—there would be three classes in a row—and saw that the next class had the same assignment, for the same play, and that the last class was going to watch part of the movie.

She checked her watch, and turned to write the questions on the board. She knew by the time she had written out the first couple of lines that she would not attempt a discussion. She didn't want to maneuver her way through the students' apathy and insolence, second-guessing who could be called on and who to avoid. She would tell the students they could work in pairs to write out answers in preparation for a discussion the next day—with their teacher. "Keep it down," she would say sternly, "or you will have to work singly, in silence." That was about the extent of her ability to threaten. That, and taking names.

Mrs. Tobler wasn't stupid; why did she leave a sub to launch talk about a boring play with a class of students who would know Maggie was a lightweight? And there were the things Mrs. Tobler had no way to know: that Maggie had no father and did not know how to talk about fathers, that her children's father was in Texas selling motorcycles, *that she had been up all night with a sick baby.*

"Cheers."

She looked up to see Rachel at the door. There were five minutes left of lunch hour. She waved at Rachel to come in. Rachel was wearing a nicely cut but loose-fitting dress, and Maggie couldn't be sure, but she thought she had lost weight. Maggie could see it in the face, where Rachel's rather delicate features had for the past year seemed buried in flesh.

"They hired a teacher from Milwaukee for that freshman slot," Rachel told her. Maggie had applied, but the truth was, she had just about forgotten there was an opening. Her application was on file—it had been on file four years, here, and in the next two towns over, except that she had skipped the year after she had Stevie. They were never going to hire her. Why should they? She had a B.A. in English and a basic teaching certificate. She had no experience other than subbing, and she was nothing special, personally. She didn't ski or play handball, she hadn't been to Thailand, she didn't speak another language, and she wasn't particularly good at teaching (not that she had had a chance to test that very far). Her only real qualification was that she would be a cheap hire. She had counted on that but it wasn't paying off.

Rachel smirked. "Milwaukee, Wisconsin, not Milwaukee, Oregon."

"Really," Maggie said, not even mildly interested.

"There's a rumor that she's black. A black teacher on this staff. Imagine that. Don't you hope she's married?"

Maggie looked up. She tried to remember the last

time she had seen a black person in Lupine, other than athletes at the college. Two years ago they had done a play at the theatre, with an all-black cast.

"It was all done by mail, by phone. She didn't come out to interview."

"And they don't know?"

"Oh, they know. But we don't know."

Maggie didn't understand why Rachel was telling her this. She asked, truly curious.

"Maggie, you are so damned literal. You remind me sometimes of Leah." Leah was Rachel's four-year old daughter.

Blood rose to Maggie's face. She felt insulted, without understanding the nature of the accusation.

Rachel saw. "Oh shit, Maggie, don't be so thin-skinned. I'm teasing you."

Maggie picked up the chalk again. "I need to write the rest of these questions out."

"What I meant was, everybody's talking about it like it matters. I was commenting on the petty, stupid nature of gossip at LHS."

Maggie set the chalk down and leaned on the desk, to give her hands someplace to be firm. "You weren't gossiping?"

"I was being *ironic*. Well, maybe not. I mean, not actual irony, in the literary sense. But *I* don't care. I hope it's true, and I think it's worth *mentioning* because it's all they're talking about in the English offices."

The first bell rang.

"Sorry," Rachel said.

"I didn't expect anything," Maggie said. "I've never been called for an interview."

"Not that. I assumed you'd know what I meant. In a way it's a compliment, you know. Thinking that you'd know. My therapist says I've become a master of hidden meaning because I don't want anyone to know my real state of mind. She says if I keep it up it will interfere with my writing. It already interferes with the integrity of my life. I ought to be better at saying things straight out."

"I suppose you could practice on me, but I'm not really the one you're hiding anything from," Maggie said, suddenly, inordinately proud of her insight. She had always considered Rachel mysterious; what if she were just deceptive?

Rachel didn't miss it. "Everybody underestimates you," she said. "Even you."

As Rachel left, Maggie wondered whether Rachel was avoiding honesty in her marriage, or in her writing—with her Muse, Rachel would say—or just with herself. Something about Rachel invited you to speculate. She was an interesting woman, and Maggie had always admired her. She didn't have time, though, to analyze her; twenty-seven high school juniors were pouring into the room.

She wrote out another question, then turned to call the roll.

The last period of the day was a free one for Mrs. Tobler, but Maggie wasn't supposed to leave until four. She tidied the two piles of papers she had collected in class, then took a paperback book out of her purse. It was a collection of short stories by women, all having to do with love and family. What *didn't* have to do with love and family? Business and war, she supposed. Did women write about those things?

A student came in and said there was a phone call for her; she could take it in the library.

She ran to take it, worried it was the baby. It was

Polly, to say that Jay's teacher had called and she needed to go over there as soon as she was free. "He seemed to think Jay's not doing so well," Polly said. "He assured me it's not an emergency. And Maggie, Stevie's feeling much better. She doesn't have any fever at all."

Maggie took her time slip down to the front office and laid it on the counter. The secretary tapped it with her long nails. "We really aren't supposed to check you out until four."

"I have to be over at the grade school."

The secretary looked at her, clearly disbelieving, but was twenty minutes worth a confrontation? She pulled the slip of paper toward her. "Mrs. Tobler will be back tomorrow, you know."

"I'm so glad," Maggie said.

The children had already cleared out of the building and the buses were gone when Maggie reached Jay's school. She walked quickly to his classroom. Jack met her at the door, took hold of her in that kind of squeezed-upper-arm grasp he had, and suggested that they go down to the office.

"What's wrong?" she demanded. His overly concerned expression alarmed her.

"Now don't worry, Maggie," he said. "There's nothing really *wrong*."

"But—his grandmother said—"

"Come, why say everything twice?"

He led her into the principal's office. The principal was a pretty, plump, very sweet woman, well-liked by everyone, and she was sporting the same damned look as Jack.

Maggie sank into the one soft chair in the office. Jack sat on a straight-backed chair a little closer to the principal's desk. Mrs. Cecil. The kids all called her Miz-C.

"Jay?" Maggie said.

"Oh, he's gone on home on the bus," Mrs. Cecil said.

"He had a hard day," Jack said.

"He's such a sweet kid," Mrs. Cecil said.

"Usually," Jack added.

"What has he done?" Maggie asked.

"It's not so much one thing—" Mrs. Cecil said, "—as it is a pattern that seems to be emerging."

"Of what?" Maggie asked.

"There was one thing today," Jack interjected.

"Jack thought it was so close to the end of the year, we could let things go by—" Mrs. Cecil began, but Jack interrupted her. He leaned toward Maggie, his arms resting on his knees.

"He sprayed a boy today, on the stage."

"Sprayed?" Maggie's immediate image was of her son peeing on someone's foot. He used to do that when he was little. On his own foot. When he first started peeing standing up. He didn't always wait for the stream to end. He was in a hurry to get away, and he'd let go too soon.

"And a little scuffle ensued," the teacher added.

"Ensued," Maggie repeated. Spoken in that isolated way, the word had an exotic sound, like a greeting in another language.

"They were working on the play for Spanish night," Jack continued.

"Mrs. Jarrett," Mrs. Cecil said. Jack stopped talking. He pulled his hands together, folded them so that they hung in a lump between his knees. "We're worried about Jay because he seems so angry. So unhappy."

"He hasn't seemed that way to me," Maggie said. It

was true, wasn't it? He was the same old Jay? Or was he unhappy, the way he slid his food around on his plate with his fork while he drooped his head? The way he holed up in the bedroom at Polly's with his comic books and didn't come out for hours? The way he refused to speak to Mo when he called? And then wouldn't talk about it. She assumed it was something he was growing into, and would grow out of.

"His dad—" Maggie said, shrugging. She was embarrassed. She didn't want to talk about Mo with her son's teacher. She didn't think it was anyone's business. Besides, she didn't know what to say.

"Divorce always affects the children," Mrs. Cecil said in a soothing, sympathetic voice, devoid of accusation.

"We're not divorced!" Maggie said. "Jay's father is out of town—on a job." She felt furious with herself for the lie—which wasn't entirely a lie but not the truth, either—and furious with these people for putting her in a position to explain. "He's in Texas," she said helplessly. She was afraid she would start to cry.

"I'm going to take him out of the Spanish play," Jack said. "It does seem clear he started the scuffle, and he has to experience some consequence—"

"If it was a scuffle, there must have been other boys—" Maggie said. Jay was a small boy, maybe the smallest in his class.

"Punam volunteered to drop out, too," Jack said. "He acknowledged that he should share the responsibility. He was trying to get the paint can away from Jay."

"The paint shouldn't have been on the stage," Mrs. Cecil said. "We'll talk about it in faculty meeting, to be sure it doesn't happen again. We want a safe environment. Anything dangerous should be used under supervision.

"Actually, Punam would be a good friend for Jay, now that Gus doesn't pay him much attention. Punam is a nice kid."

Maggie, thoroughly confused, sat mute.

"I'm apologizing to you, Mrs. Jarrett," Mrs. Cecil said. "For our failure in this matter. The lack of supervision. Not calling you sooner."

"We're going to talk about it in circle tomorrow," Jack said. "You could come. You could talk to Jay about that."

Maggie shook her head vigorously. "No no," she said. "I couldn't."

"Parents often sit in," Mrs. Cecil said.

Maggie shook her head again.

"We have to talk about the roughhousing on the stage," Jack said. "And we have to talk about what to do when we're angry."

"The children are very close," Mrs. Cecil said. "And Jennifer will be sitting in."

"Jennifer?"

"Jennifer is our child development specialist. This is her first year on staff. We got her, you know, because so many parents lobbied the Board. Parents can't bear all the load."

Maggie, ashamed, feeling tears on the way, put her face in her hands.

"Mrs. Jarrett," Mrs. Cecil said, rising from her chair.

"The—baby—is—sick," Maggie whimpered. It was simply more than she could stand.

Mrs. Cecil pulled up another chair and sat close to Maggie.

"This isn't a terribly serious matter," she said gently.

"It's just that we like for the parents to know what's going on in the child's classroom. We want you to understand that we care about *Jay*, and not just about his reading and math."

Maggie shook her head, but she still wouldn't look up. She felt Mrs. Cecil's hand lie lightly on her forearm.

Jack said, "Excuse me, Maggie. I'll talk to you later in the week."

She heard him go.

"It must be very hard for you right now," Mrs. Cecil said.

Maggie slid her hands down so that the tips of her fingers were over her mouth. She looked up into the principal's face. Then she bent her head forward, tipping toward her. Mrs. Cecil's arms came up. For just a moment, Maggie didn't worry, or think at all. She simply folded into the principal's warm embrace.

"They didn't say anything about this!" Maggie said when she saw Jay's face. There was a bruise on his cheek. He wouldn't answer any of her questions. They were in Polly's living room. Maggie held Stevie in her lap and outwaited her son.

"I got socked with the paint can," Jay said finally. "It doesn't hurt."

Polly was across the room, in the kitchen, making chicken-fried steak. Her back was to them.

"Can I go now?" Jay whined.

"Oh honey," Maggie said. She couldn't bear his misery.

He headed for the kitchen door.

"You're having supper with me," Polly said.

He turned and looked at his mother pleadingly.

Maggie looked to Polly, but her mother-in-law was back at the stove.

Maggie, after a huge sigh which turned into an even bigger yawn, said, "I'll call you when supper's ready."

"I don't want to eat," Jay said. He stood with the sliding door open, one foot in, one foot out of the kitchen.

Polly turned around, her finger on her nose. It was an eccentric gesture she used unconsciously when she was suppressing admonition. As soon as the door was closed, she left the stove and joined Maggie on the couch. Stevie stirred, then opened her eyes and began to cry. Polly reached over to stroke the back of her head.

"Oh Polly, I made such a fool of myself," Maggie said. "I actually cried in the principal's office." She didn't say: in the principal's arms.

"It doesn't seem so bad," Polly said.

"They said there's a whole pattern."

"Of what?"

"He doesn't finish his work. He bugs other kids."

Stevie began to cry more earnestly. Polly had to get up and mind the food on the stove. Maggie moved to the rocking chair and soothed the baby. Rocking made them both feel better.

"If I were you," Polly said from the kitchen, "I'd keep Jay home tomorrow and spend some time with him. Go for a hike or something. A bike ride. Let him sleep in. In fact, why don't you let Stevie stay the night, and you can sleep in, too?"

It sounded so good.

Jay slipped open the door. "It's Dad on the phone," he said.

"He could call me here," Maggie said. She'd like for Polly to be on hand, for Mo to know she was.

"He says come right now," Jay said. "He says he wants to talk to you out there."

Polly held her arms out for Stevie. Jay turned and ran back to the cottage. Maggie followed slowly.

Jay was holding the phone out in front of him. She took it from him. "I was in the house with your mother," she said.

"Where else?" Mo said. Maggie nearly hung up right then, but Jay stood in the middle of the room, watching her, his expression—hurt? lonesome? confused? *eager?*—so needy and expectant *and so like her own*, she gripped the receiver and took a long breath through her nose.

"Did you get my letter?" he said.

It had come that day. It lay unread on the arm of her sofa.

"Stevie's sick. We were up all night," she heard herself say. "Jay's been in trouble at school."

Jay made a small, startled sound, and ran out of the cottage.

"Sick with what? Has she been to the doctor?"

"I'm too tired to talk," she said.

"You haven't read it, have you?"

"I just got home. I had to go see Jay's teacher."

"Let me talk to Jay."

"He's outside." She sniffed, ready to cry for the second time today.

"Jerry's opening a second shop. I'm going to manage this one."

"Great."

"Maggie, it's a real job, and I like it. Please, Maggie. Hang up and read my letter. You can call me back. You have the number there, don't you? I'll be home all night."

She knew he would hear the tears in her voice. "I've got to go."

"You have to tell me what's going on."

"We thought she'd swallowed something!" she burst out. "I thought she was choking. Polly took us to the hospital."

"You weren't going to call me?"

"She's making supper, I've got to go."

"*Maggie.* We're not talking about my mother, we're talking about us."

"I owe the hospital seventy dollars," she said.

"I'll send it in the morning." He sounded flat and sad. "What about Jay?"

"I couldn't do it without Polly."

"You could do it with me," he said. "I love you. You love me, don't you?"

"There are too many things to think about here. I can't think about you." She felt a burning pain just under her ribs. It hurt so much she bent over.

"I'll call tomorrow. I'll call every day. Read my letter, please."

She couldn't think what to say, but she could hardly believe it when he hung up.

She did read his letter. It made her cry. Then she went in to talk to Polly.

Polly was just hanging up the phone herself. She set it in the cradle and turned as Maggie came into the kitchen. Maggie had Mo's letter in her hand.

Polly looked happy, her whole body poised, her

hands in the air in front of her, that bustling, ready look she had sometimes, when there were things to accomplish.

"The baby is coming day after tomorrow!" she said. "A little girl."

Maggie stared. Her arms hung at her side, and Mo's letter brushed her hip.

"Supper's about ready, dear. Want to call Jay?"

Maggie took the letter back to her cottage and laid it on her bed. Outside, she called Jay, but he didn't answer. When she was quiet, though, she heard sounds by the garage.

He was sitting on the ground, crying. His face was hidden in his arms. She knelt beside him. As she did, she saw something was broken on the ground in front of him.

"What's this?" She picked up a shard. It looked like a piece from a mug.

Without looking up, he sniffed and said, "It's my Garfield cup."

She moved over by him and slid her arm across his back.

"I don't understand, honey." She saw the other pieces. She could tell they had been here a while. Most of the pieces were crusted with dirt.

Mo had given Jay the cup and the T-shirt for Christmas.

"I broke it when he left," Jay said. "I smashed it against the garage."

Her heart felt squeezed inside her chest. "But you wear the shirt."

He finally looked up. "I was used to it."

December 1982

* * *

"Shh." Maggie holds her finger to her lips, looking back at Mo behind her in the doorway. The house is dark, so her roommate is already asleep. Mo pulls her finger to his own lips, and kisses it. Funny melting feelings run down her, from her earlobes to her toenails.

The tiny house has a small bedroom below, and a loft above. To get to the loft, which is Maggie's, they have to climb steep stairs. They scamper up giddily, eager for the hour ahead.

Maggie sheds her black skirt and white blouse. She waits tables four nights a week at a Chinese restaurant near the college, where she takes three freshman courses: English Composition, American History, and Biology. She is eager to get past these first hurdles, which seem like high school over again. She wants to be an upperclassman, and read Shakespeare and Hemingway. She is planning to be a teacher. Polly approves, saying she will be good at it, it will be a good career. This means a lot to Maggie.

They undress, kneeling because there isn't enough headroom to stand up on the loft. Moonlight makes a long ray across the mattress and shines on their legs. It is cold in the house—they keep the heat off, or down, as much as possible, to save money—and beads of moisture have collected on the window. Maggie slides under the blankets, and as she lies back on the pillow, she sees the fat moon just beyond some trees. She reaches out and touches the wet pane. She wonders if he will give her a Christmas present. It doesn't matter; she has never been this happy. She has never had a boyfriend that mattered, though she did let one show her how It's done, her senior year.

Mo, beside her, moves his leg over hers and presses his knee into her groin. They are perfectly matched, she thinks. He is small, like her, with fine bones and a smooth pale chest. When he kisses her, she feels how well their bodies suit one another, how their warmth goes back and forth, and then inside her, lush, sweet, hot.

"I'm going to come back, you know," he says.

"I hope so!" she says, her gaiety forced. "You do live here."

He has been away, in the army, in Texas. He is a mechanic. He's home on Christmas leave.

"Mom told me over and over how special you are," he whispers.

She shivers, thinking of Polly. "Oh, what would she say?" she asks. She doesn't want him to go; she doesn't want his mother to know.

"I've never had a special girl," he says into her ear.

March 1983

* * *

Over spring break, she took a bus all the way to his base in Texas. They had three days. They stayed in a motel. She couldn't get over how nice it was. The glasses were wrapped in a waxy paper. The bathroom was spacious, with a deep tub and lots of hot water. She took two baths every day. She washed her hair and Mo combed it while she sat on the bed wrapped up in towels.

They went to a bar where there was a band and dancing. He loved to dance. He had learned steps there that went with the Texas music. They carded her, so she drank Cokes all evening. Mo drank beer. Still, she felt high and happy. She was pretty good at the "stomp" by the time they left.

There were two beds in the motel room. They made love in one and then moved to the clean one. As she was falling asleep, she thought about Mo's bed at home, in the Jarretts' house. She remembered how bare the room had been when she arrived.

She thought about him sleeping in that bed when he was home on leave, maybe on sheets she had slept on lots of times.

She tucked her face under the edge of the sheet; she wanted to smell their smells after making love.

The second night, they went to a carnival and rode

the ferris wheel. They took their pictures together in a tiny booth, and divided them up.

It was May before she wrote to tell him she was pregnant. She was so afraid. She thought he would think she planned it, but they'd used condoms, it was an accident, it was meant to be.

"I haven't told your mother," she wrote. She was scared. Polly meant the world to her, what would she think?

Mo called the night he got the letter. He said he wasn't sure how soon he could get home, but not to worry. We'll tell her together, he said.

What will she say? she asked. It was confusing, to be so scared and happy at the same time.

She'll say, welcome to the family, he told her. He wrote her a long letter, saying that he loved her. He said it couldn't have worked out better.

May 1992

* * *

When Dulce returns to the trailer and finds that Gus has not come home—he will have gone off with Hilario—she moves about the tiny space, picking up clothes, washrags, bowls and cups. There is no room for the casual clutter of a house. There is space only for the essentials. Dulce resists whatever they can do without. Gus says they are the only family in the whole country without a television. All Dulce can say is it seems unnecessary. She doesn't want the noise. She loves long quiet evenings with her son. She sits on the kitchen chair, her chin on her knees, and watches him read. He looks up and catches her and frowns, but when he goes back to his book he lets his grin show. She turns to the table and opens her notebook, running her finger down the lines where her dreams are written.

Gus has left a mess from morning, making his lunch. She woke him as she left, but he turned over with a groan and probably got up late. She doesn't mind. She cleans the lid of the peanut jar and screws it on tight, wipes the breadboard and props it against the wall, and picks up the empty bread bag. As she crumples it, she suddenly remembers standing in a tiny space like this, a girl of five, working before dawn to make sandwiches for her father, his brother, and her mother, while her mother made breakfast. It was a scalding summer in the Midwest—Michigan?—their last migrant season before they came to Oregon and stayed. Get up, Dulcita, her mother would say, it's time. And then, with the sky barely light, they were away to the fields, and Dulce back in bed to sleep, and later to play with a sock doll her mother had made, and sleep more, and wait.

As Dulce recalls herself at five, she envies the small child with her morning responsibility, and the pleasure of her parents' return for supper, then the night in the one-room cabin, the three of them in one bed, her uncle on a cot.

She throws the bread bag away and goes to the other side of the partition to lie on her bed. Gustavo's letter is tucked between the pillow and the wall. It rustles as she puts her head on the pillow.

She dreams of a boy and a girl in an orange grove. They sit under a tree and eat the fruit, waiting until the trees are shadowy and frightening, and the sky has lost its light. They clasp hands and creep through the grove, listening for the sounds of animals, listening for their parents' calls. They hear other children singing, but when they get toward the voices, their direction is lost. Papa! the little boy calls. Mama! calls the girl. Then, as they are exhausted and hopeless, they stumble into a clearing. There is a hut, and smoke from a fire. Carefully, slowly, they creep toward the hut. The door is ajar. Inside, the fire lights and warms the room. A rough wooden table is laid with food: heaping bowls of beans, a plate of pan dulce, shiny, slippery peppers in bowls. They sit. Bowls and spoons are already at their places.

But whose hut is it? Who lives here, and where are they? Eat, the little girl says. She has Dulce's face.

When she awakes, it is nearly seven. She sits up, not quite alarmed, but disturbed to find herself still alone. She knows Gus feels more and more at home at the Hinojosas'; she knows he likes the bustle and chatter, the presence of children. She tries not to mind. Lupe treats Gus and her son Hilario like small men, especially now, with Hilario's father away in Mexico. But Gus is only nine—nearly ten—and he is *her* son, and what she does mind is waking in the near-dark to find him gone.

She takes out her notebook and looks back through old pages. The dream of the children in the orange grove: she has had it before. Sometimes they hear a woman singing. Sometimes they see a deep, lidded pot on the stove. Sometimes they hear footsteps outside the door, and spring from their seats, calling, Papa!

She closes the book again. The boy, of course, is Gus. Why should she dream that they are lost?

It doesn't matter. Dulce believes in her dreams, not as portents or metaphors, but as separate experiences, valid and wholly sensate. She knows that the life of her dreams is another life quite apart from her ordinary dailiness. Her dreams are a deeper, more mysterious, yet simpler life. They keep her sane. Even when they disturb her, they seem fine. She writes them down, not to analyze them, but to savor, and record. She does not wish to scare her dreams away, or complicate them. She does not mind that they are outside of her control. She understands that dreams are a kind of salvation. They are the way she holds to the parts of her that would otherwise be lost. Most of the time they are in Spanish—if there are words—and thus it is in dreams that she maintains her identity. Dreams are her culture.

She brushes at the wrinkles in her skirt, then splashes her face at the kitchen sink. She goes to her car, and thinks about going over to Lupe's, the pleasure on Lupe's face: oh comadre, she'll say, come in and I will give you a cold drink. She'll put her in the one soft chair, near the table she uses as an altar, covered with a crocheted throw, a statue of the Virgin, a picture of the Sacred Heart, votive candles and rosaries and holy cards, postcard photos of a cathedral in Mexico City. The babies will try to crawl onto Dulce's lap, and she will kiss their fat cheeks and say how fast they're growing. In a little while, she'll ask what Lupe needs, this woman in a trailer with no hot water, four children, an absent husband, no English, and complete faith in the will of God.

It makes Dulce so tired, she leans her forehead against the steering wheel and sighs. She wonders if the school meant this to happen, if someone said, why we'll put this big Mexican boy in Gus Quirarte's class so that they can look out for one another, for who else should? They stand out, two dark broad-faced boys with shiny straight hair, though Hilario is a head taller. And it's true, the boys have grown so close they seem to be excluding everyone else, and Lupe has grown fervently attached to Dulce, who, after all, speaks English, is a citizen, knows her way around. Has a car.

For the Hinojosas are illegal, and Lupe will not—cannot—ask anyone in the government for help. She works several afternoons a week at a laundromat, paid "under the table." She cleans each pot of beans she feeds her family to the last morsel. They live in a trailer on a lot near the freeway exit, behind the filling station where her husband Cipriano has worked since their truck broke down in February, passing through Lupine on the way to California from Christmas tree planting. Only Cipriano has gone to Chihuahua to see his sick mother, and all that Dulce can think is, maybe he won't come back. She wonders if Lupe wouldn't be better off in Chihuahua, too, but when she asked why they didn't all go, Lupe said, it is too hard to cross. It is too hard to come back, and we are already here.

As she puts the key into the ignition, she looks up and sees her son loping across the intersection toward the trailer court. He is with Hilario. At the corner, only two car lengths away, the boys pause, give one another a slap of palms in the air above their heads, and Hilario runs back toward home. Dulce watches, and sees how her son swaggers, a child imitating a man. She is about to call out to him when she hears his name, sees Hilario turned again, gesturing for him to come. She watches Gus run across the street, where Hilario is leaning into a low-slung car parked at the curb. Horrified, she sees the boys open the car doors and slide in. She jumps out of her car and runs over to them. Hilario's hands are on the steering wheel. She hears him as she reaches the car. Vroom! vroom! he says. Gus is laughing, and bangs on the dashboard.

She jerks open the door and slaps her hand on her son's shoulder. "Get out of there!" she shouts. Both boys are instantly silent, shocked, turned to stare at her. "What do you think you're doing!" she screeches. Her hand is clamped on his arm.

"Mom!" he protests, shoving at her hand. "Okay, okay." He crawls out, pushing against her body, as Hilario gets out the other side. "Es nada," Hilario says. "We don't do nothing." He tries to laugh. "A yoke," he mispronounces. He looks at her with the native, jocular insolence of a cocky young man. Already he knows women will defer to him.

"Go home!" she says sharply. He shrugs, turns, and runs away.

To her son, she says, "Where were you?" though she knows.

She marches him across the street. By her car, she pauses. Her chest hurts. She realizes that, in fact, they were doing nothing, boys acting silly in an unlocked car. She puts her hands on her son's arm again. Intently, she looks at him and she says, "You have to understand. Two Mexican boys in someone's car. It doesn't matter that it was nothing. You would get in so much trouble."

"Mom, we knew the car. It's Mr. Nathan's car. The P.E. teacher. What would he do to us? He left it unlocked. We weren't hurting it."

She makes herself take a deep breath, takes her hands away. She points to her car. "Get in.

"Did you eat?" she asks. He presses himself against the far door. He mumbles something about a tamale.

"What? What were you doing?"

They were watching the little kids while Lupe was at the laundromat. She left tamales.

"I haven't eaten," Dulce says.

He sits up. "I'm still hungry."

"I heard from your father," she says. She didn't know she was going to say that. "From Texas."

His head jerks up. "What's he want, Mom? Is he coming?"

"He wants you—us—he wants us to come to Texas. To his folks."

"When, Mama? We will go, won't we?"

"I don't know. I don't know."

"Does it cost too much? On the bus?"

"He sent money."

"I want to go!"

"I don't know yet. School's not out. We'll see then. In June."

"There are ways to get to Texas," he says sulkily. It's a dare. She has told him how her papa walked the last forty miles to the border, to save his pesos for the crossing, his first time.

"I haven't made any supper," she says. "We could go for hamburgers."

He shrugs. She knows he wants to go.

She reaches for his hand. "Let's get through the school year," she says. "You know how I am about you missing school."

He pulls his hand away and gets quickly out of the car and runs to the trailer. Sighing, she pulls away from the curb. She'll get food and bring it back. She'll tell him she knows he wants his father, though she wonders what he thinks that means. She will say he isn't big enough to go all that way on the bus, but she knows he can do it, knows, too, that sooner or later he will. She will try not to think how that will break her heart.

After supper the four of them—Polly, Maggie, and the children—lined up cozily on the couch to watch videos of cartoon movies. Jay slumped against his mother and played the little boy, until some idle gesture of affection on her part reminded him he was unhappy, and he inched away. Stevie, seated on her other side, pointed and called out "Mousie!" about a hundred times, whatever the nature of the characters. Polly, benign, put on her bifocals and worked a crossword puzzle, no doubt relieved at the relative peace.

Later, Jay took his comic books to bed down the hall. Maggie bathed Stevie, getting in the tub with her, taking a long time, making a game of soaping and washing and rinsing. When Stevie was in her crib and quiet, Maggie went in to see Jay. She sat on the bed and put her hand on his knee over the covers. His cheek where the can had struck him was purple. He made a show of turning the page of a comic book—all his comics starred great hulking powerful men and dastardly villains capable of shocking crimes—and not wanting to be disturbed. Maggie sat quietly.

Mo's boyhood room, where she had lived for three years, had been changed a couple of times since then. As Mo's father grew more and more ill with lung cancer, Polly stripped the room of its girlish frills, bought new green sheets, and installed him there to die. Maggie couldn't help thinking of her suspicions about the room that day of her arrival. More recently, she and Gretchen had painted the room a pleasant peach color and hung posters of art by Matisse, Balthus and Gauguin. Little by little, Jay had deposited various toys and books in the room. He slept there often, times his mother stayed late talking with Polly or watching TV, or because he wanted to be in a room of his own. He knew it had been his father's room. "Did Dad have his bed like this?" he'd asked more than once. "Where did

Granny put all of Dad's toys?" he asked another time. (The answer: the garage. Most of them, however, had been hauled out for Jay himself as a smaller boy.)

"Would you like to skip school tomorrow?" Maggie asked.

He glanced up, surprised, then tamped down his pleasure. "Whatever."

"I thought you could sleep in. I want to keep an eye on your eye." She smiled. It did sound funny. He didn't get it, though. He didn't so much as blink. "And if you want, we could go for a hike or a ride or something. How does that sound?"

She could see he wanted to be enthusiastic but wouldn't allow her the pleasure.

"Okay."

"Honey, is there something you want to say?"

The sadness of his expression made her throat constrict. Then he tossed his comic book to the end of the bed and crawled down under the covers.

"Would you like to call Dad tomorrow?"

He flopped over, his back to her. "What for?" he said, his words muffled by the covers.

"Sleep tight," she said. She didn't know what else to say.

Polly was watching a movie starring Doris Day and Rock Hudson. "Silly, aren't they?" she said, but it was clear she was enjoying it. Maggie kissed her goodnight and went to Gretchen's room. The big bed was piled with pillows and stuffed animals, quilts and magazines, shed clothing and brochures from wilderness travel agencies. Maggie fluffed pillows, folded the clothes, arranged the magazines on the bedside stand, and crawled in to wait for Gretchen. The theatre was dark tonight, and Maggie assumed she'd gone to Blake's for what must be very close to the last night they would have before their ninety-day love affair came to a halt.

Poor Gretchen, she thought, making herself comfortable against the pillows. She should have stuck with the river guide last summer, the one who ate gorp and built his own sweat lodge.

She got back up and fetched a tattered copy of *The Golden Notebook* from Gretchen's bookshelf. How she had struggled to read it for her book group last year! The discussion had been a volley between Nora and Rachel (politics and sex), until Lynn said she found Lessing humorless, and could they move on to something contemporary, please? Through it all, Maggie was thrilled to be there. She still thought it was amazing to have been asked to join such a clever group.

As she was mulling over these things, weariness overcame her and she fell asleep with the light on. She was still lying like that when Gretchen came home around midnight.

"Doris Lessing!" Gretchen picked up the book and waved it over Maggie's face. "No wonder you were sleeping deeply." She laughed and tossed the book to a corner of the room. Maggie didn't think the laugh sounded merry.

"You know what one of the actors said to me at the lounge last night?" she asked Maggie as she changed into pajamas. "He said, 'Gretchen, you are looking wan.' I laughed, of course, so he laughed too, but he felt sorry for me, you could see it in his eyes." She slid under the covers. "Do you think everyone knows what an ass I've made of myself, fucking Phoebe Alex's husband?"

"I never thought actors were prudes." Maggie envied Gretchen her job, which had opened up the very day Polly called in her cards after twenty years of volunteering at the theatre.

"I suppose they're not," Gretchen said, lying back and staring straight up at the ceiling. Maggie remembered that there were fluorescent dots up there, a rendering of a summer's night sky. She didn't think Gretchen was ready for the dark yet, though.

"I was at Blake's."

"I thought you might spend the night," Maggie said, though she was glad Gretchen had come home. It felt very sisterly to lie in bed and talk until sleep overcame them. They had done so hundreds of times over the years. They'd lain right here and sobbed half the night before Gretchen married dreadful Mark and went off to Alaska for two years.

She would tell Gretchen about Mo's letter and they would talk until she figured out what she felt about it.

"We weren't at the apartment. He's moved everything out. We went to the new house."

"No!" The new house was Phoebe Alex's house, and she would be in it any day now, arriving in Lupine from six months on location in Mexico.

"He took me around to show me all the rooms, the deck in the moonlight, the kitchen. It has an island with a granite top. A pink sink." Gretchen turned over onto her stomach and propped herself up on her elbows. "He didn't have a bed yet. We were on some quilts on the floor. Then, while I was dressing, he lay there staring at me. 'What?' I asked him. He didn't say anything. Couldn't he say he's sorry? He thinks he's said everything. Phoebe is his wife. Phoebe needs him. He's a stage manager for chrissake! What does she need him for? They're not in graduate school anymore. She's a movie star."

"An actress, anyway," Maggie said, bored. She'd heard this a lot lately.

"She's going to be a star, all right. This movie has all the chemistry, I hear. And not from him. I hear some of the actors talking. She's got nude scenes. Imagine that—being naked with a man all over you while a crew watches. God."

"Maybe he does love her."

Gretchen fell onto her back again. "Do you ever think how many times we've been here, talking about our lives?"

"I remember speculating what would happen if a boy put his penis in and it got caught." Maggie hoped she had successfully changed the subject. "I remember asking you if you were sure about Mark."

"Don't rub it in," Gretchen said, but not crossly. Whatever bad feelings she had about Unalakleet were old and forgotten. Since then she had sewn polarlite vests for Patagonia, in California. She'd been a waitress in Aspen. She'd come home to her mother, her childhood bed, her best friend.

"I remember asking you what your brother was like. Before I ever met him." It was pointless, but Maggie realized suddenly that what she wanted to do was tell Gretchen everything she already knew: how she rode the bus to Texas and fell in love with Mo. How everything came together in her life when Jay was born. "He wrote me an amazing letter," she whispered. "I don't know what to make of it."

"I can't believe he hasn't told her," Gretchen said, as if Maggie hadn't spoken at all. "They go ahead as if everything is the same as it ever was. Is that possible?

Have I been dreaming? He's put a birdfeeder on the deck. Their furniture arrives from L.A. tomorrow. The house has this thirty-dollar-a-yard carpet they'll have to pay someone to vacuum every other day." Inevitably, she started to cry.

Maggie whispered, in return. "Polly's new baby is a girl. She heard this morning. They're bringing her Wednesday. A baby with special needs. What can that mean? All babies have special needs. Sometimes they don't go away. What about Jay? I can't believe the way he looks at me. What about Stevie? Does Polly hope we'll disappear? Is all this so I'll have to go to Texas?"

Gretchen sighed noisily. "He tells me, 'you knew it all along.' I hate him when he says that. We've been lovers for three months. Okay I knew, like I know about the ozone layer. Like I know about taxes. It threatens, but it's abstract. I saw her in *Retribution*. It wasn't great, but she's a movie star. What does she want with Blake? Why does she want a house in Lupine?"

Maggie said, "I didn't really think he'd go without me. Why does he want to live so far away from home? Doesn't he understand that kids need family? They talk funny in Texas. A letter's not enough, not when he's not even sorry about leaving. What does he think marriage is?"

"If anyone said to me the whole thing is just sex, I'd bust them in their loud mouth. Bust *her*, I guess."

"It's a lot more than sex. It's everything." Finally, they were talking about the same thing.

"Mo thought you'd go, you know. Right up to the last minute. So did I. It was double-dare. You should go, what's here?"

Maggie switched off the light. Stars twinkled on the

ceiling. She and Gretchen had put them there their senior year in high school, using a paper stencil. She could make out Cassiopeia.

Maybe they would talk tomorrow. She moved close to Gretchen. "Blake has a weak chin," she said.

Gretchen snickered. "He's pathetic. I'm pathetic."

"Join the club," Maggie said.

Gretchen moaned and tossed so, Maggie moved out to her own bed in the cottage sometime in the night. Mo woke her at seven.

"I worried about Stevie all night," he said.

"She's fine." Maggie was still sleepy, and glad the call wasn't one of the schools. "We're all still in bed," she said, though she didn't know whether her children were awake or not.

"Sorry."

"It's okay."

"I get an early start, while it's cool. The mornings are pretty."

"I'm keeping Jay home today. We'll do something. He seems so moody, I thought maybe he'd talk to me."

"I feel torn in half, Maggie. I want to come home, it's crazy being away from you. But the job is great. Austin's great."

"I don't want to do this now. I'm not all the way awake."

"Yeah. Well." Both of them sour again. But Mo said, "I'm going to come up sometime in the summer. If you don't come here, I mean."

"Jay misses you a lot."

"And we'll figure it out then."

"If it can be figured out." Her same old stubbornness was stiffening her neck. "This is home, Mo. This is where we live." Why couldn't he understand?

"I'm not going to argue on the phone."

"What's to argue about?"

"Only our lives. All four of us."

"I'm going back to sleep."

"Maggie. Don't hang up mad."

"What's the use, Mo?"

"The *use* is only everything. The *use* is we have two kids and *I love you.*"

Maggie gulped. "I love you too," she said, but very quietly. She hung up before he could make too much of it.

Jay stumbled out to eat cereal about nine, then went back to bed. Maggie looked to Polly for a hint of what to do with him, but Polly was writing out bills. Maggie had already had breakfast with her, and fed Stevie, and was finding it difficult to keep from brooding about Mo's phone call. She was relieved when Polly said she had to dig some things out of the garage to get ready for the new baby.

Polly brought in an old crib, and Maggie scrubbed it while Polly went off for a tin of paint. They moved it out onto the patio and painted it white with a turquoise trim. In a burst of creativity, Maggie drew tiny flowers on the headboard. She could feel Polly's pleasure and excitement building. Babies.

"What do you know about the baby?" she asked her.

Polly said she was the child of an addicted mother, and wasn't going to be easy at first. Maggie chewed on her lip. She could see it now: Polly rocking and walking an infant, Gretchen pouting and playing poor-me recluse, Maggie and her kids suddenly odd ones out. Polly was humming to herself. The sunshine gleamed on her short black hair. "Kendra," she said.

Jay wandered out, still in his pj's, rubbing his eyes. He went straight to Polly for a hug, glowering at his mother. Maggie felt a twinge of envy and hurt. "How about a real breakfast now?" she asked, trying to sound cheerful. She had read somewhere that if you refused to let your child cloud your spirits, he learned—what? She couldn't remember, and she couldn't imagine. She felt what he felt, not the other way around. He clung to Polly, who extricated herself and patted him on the back. "I've got a little more to do here, Jay-Jay, but you could fry some bacon if you like." Jay looked at his mother, his chin up.

"I'll make some cinnamon toast," Maggie said. "Stevie loves it." Stevie, hearing her name, ran across the patio and flung herself at Maggie.

Sometimes children are like great huge sacks of flour to be lugged and handled and lifted and kept. Sometimes Maggie would like to close her eyes and think there was nobody out there who needed her.

"I like it too," Jay said.

"Then why don't you help me make it?" Surely they could manage that. Making a mess was always therapeutic.

After breakfast they played a board game, Space Agents. It was the simplest of games—roll the dice and move—but he loved it. He thought being an astronaut was a real possibility. They played until Maggie's space ship got ahead of Jay's for the third time and he accused her of cheating.

"Cheating!" She couldn't believe the anger that

flashed in his eyes. "I rolled the dice and counted the moves, you watched me all the time." She didn't know why she was arguing with him. His anger had nothing to do with Space Agents. She felt a nauseating wave of helplessness. She didn't know what she was supposed to do to make him feel better. What was so terrible, anyway? She doubted half the kids in his school lived with both parents. It wasn't like his dad was dead.

They exchanged more words, silly words between a child and his mother, and then Jay stood up abruptly and tipped the board off the ottoman and sent the pieces flying onto the floor. When he saw what he had done, he squeezed his eyes into ugly slits. "I hate Space Agents!" he cried. "It's a boring baby game."

Stevie was grabbing pieces in her little fists, and Maggie was trying to watch that she didn't eat them or toss them under furniture. She wasn't really looking at Jay.

Jay kicked at the board, and though his kick didn't hurt anything, it scared Stevie and made her howl, and shocked Maggie, who lunged for him and barely caught his sleeve, then lost it as he turned. He ran down the hall and slammed the bedroom door behind him.

Polly was standing in the kitchen doorway. Maggie began crying, which escalated Stevie's distress. Polly came over and sat down on the floor beside the baby. "There, there," she said. Maggie glared at the both of them. What about me? she wanted to say. Gretchen appeared at the end of the hall and asked what the *hell* was going on, then turned and slammed *her* door.

Maggie threw herself on the couch and sobbed.

The day was beautiful. The sun shone. The temperature was in the mid-seventies. The lightest breeze blew. They couldn't stay unhappy.

"I have an idea," Polly said a little before three. "Why don't you take Jay for an ice cream? Stevie and I will walk down to the park for a bit. How's that sound?"

Gretchen, glowering and speechless, had already dressed and made it out of the house. She hosted the members' lounge before the matinee. Wouldn't she be the gracious one today?

Jay seemed to perk up at the suggestion, and Maggie, her eyes stinging, agreed that ice cream sounded good. They headed off for the Dairy Queen.

"Tell you what," she said when they were in the alcove to the store. "You get me a single cone, vanilla. And you can have whatever you want." She handed him a five dollar bill.

He looked at it as if he didn't know what it was.

"I'll get a seat," she said. She thought he looked pleased, once he figured out what he was doing. They went inside and he moved into line behind some other kids.

Only he backed away, one step, then another and another, until he had backed against the counter where the newspapers were spread out. Maggie hurried over to him. He looked ready to cry.

"What now!" she said. He pointed, the tiniest gesture.

She saw then that the boys in front of him were Hilario and Gus. Gus gave him a little wave, then said something in Spanish to Hilario, who snickered. They left.

"What?" Maggie asked Jay, exasperated.

Jay thrust the bill into her hand. "I don't want any."

"What did they say? What did they do?"

"Nothing! They didn't say nothing to me."

She followed him out to the car. She made herself sit in silence. She would outlast him. She would make him say what was wrong. In a moment he said, "I should have gone to school. I missed practice for Spanish night."

"You're not in Spanish night, Jay. Jack said. You know he said. Because of the paint can." God, she hated Jack!

He turned his head and hung his chin on the window. "I hate Jack," he said quietly.

"Jay." She touched his arm lightly, but he yanked it away.

"I talked to your dad this morning. He's going to come up."

He swung around. "He's coming back?"

"He's coming to—to see you."

When he didn't say anything to that, she started the car. She pulled out into the street in the direction away from home. Maybe if they drove around a bit they would both calm down.

She drove past the high school, a mistake, she soon saw, because buses were loading and students were crossing the street any place they liked. She slowed to a crawl.

"Let's go to Dad's place," Jay said. He'd pulled himself up in the seat.

"What, honey?" She didn't know where he meant.

He pointed down the street. "You know, down by the freeway."

"Oh, the Gabrelli property. Okay." She was relieved to get past the high school throng. In a couple more blocks they had crossed the back artery street and hit a poorly kept road that would deadend along the bank of the freeway.

She parked on the shoulder of the road in front of the Gabrelli place. It didn't look like anyone was there. The Gabrellis were Californians, and didn't spend much of the year here. They had bought an old farm house to renovate, and Mo had worked for a month last summer clearing the property of brush and trash, checking and steadying the old shed they wanted to keep for its blue tin roof and look of groovy old times. He had taken Jay out with him most afternoons. There was an irrigation ditch along the back of the property, fruit trees, berry bushes, several abandoned cars. It was like country, so close in.

They walked up the gravel drive past the house. There wasn't any sign of life. "We're trespassing, you know," Maggie said. Jay paid no attention. Who would care? Maybe the neighbors, but probably not. The property was three-and-a-half or four acres, the house shaded on both sides with large poplars. And they weren't hurting anything.

Behind the house the property inclined sharply, and then opened onto a rolling meadow. What was left of a shed or small barn lay low to the ground. Someone, at some time, had taken the roof right off the shed and set it on the ground, but because the roof was high-peaked, there was still room to walk beneath it. Jay headed straight there.

He knelt down by a broken concrete slab and poked at the ground. Maggie asked him what he was looking for.

"Chipmunks. Sometimes Dad and me would go to lunch and bring back french fries and they'd eat them, one at a time." He stood up abruptly. "They're not there," he said curtly, but as he walked away he looked around and his expression brightened.

Just before the opening to the shed there was a hillock of ferns. He said, "Watch, Mom!" then turned and flung himself backwards onto the mound. Spread-eagled, he lay nested in the soft foliage and smiled at her. "Come on," he said. "It's soft as pillows."

She thought about the green stains on his white T-shirt, and she thought about what might be crawling in the grass. She shook her head.

He sat up. "What'd we come for?" he said, but he headed into the ruins of the shed.

Maggie followed him under the roof, climbing over old beams and odd hunks of lumber. Near the middle of the length of it was an open place in the roof, and in the ground where the light hit, grass and a few sprigs of violets had sprung up. Someone had been here fairly recently—there were the sooty remains of a small fire, and an empty pork and beans can.

"Look, Mom!" Jay said, digging at the little mound of ashes with a stick.

"That's not very smart," Maggie said. "Dry as it is around here."

"Oh *Mom*."

She sat on a beam. The sun shone on her face and felt fine. She closed her eyes and didn't pay any attention to her son as he poked around. When she looked up again, she didn't see him. For a moment she was alarmed, then saw through the other end of the shed that he had gone out on the grass. She followed. The sun was bright in her eyes. He darted towards her, holding a long skinny branch. "Halt and surrender!" he cried.

"Put that down!" She batted at the piece of wood. "You could put my eye out."

He threw the stick on the ground and stomped on it. It cracked loudly. "Fuck," he said.

"What did you say?" She grabbed his arm.

He wrenched away. "When I come here with Dad it's fun!" he cried. "We play knights and lances. We made rosehip tea once."

"Well, your dad isn't here now," she said, sorry as soon as she said it. She marched off toward the road again, hoping he was behind her.

"Girls are babies," he said when they paused by the car. "Scared of everything. Even a little twig."

She bit her lip and got in the car. "I'm not girls," she said when he was in, too. "I'm your mother."

"Too bad," Jay said. He was just a boy, he was angry, he was grabbing for the first thing to say. Maggie knew all that, but it still made her want to cry.

"Fasten your belt," she said sharply.

Instead, he crawled over the car seat with a thud and settled in the back. At Polly's house, they headed for separate bedrooms. Stevie, who had been in the living room with Polly, toddled down to Maggie's door. She tried the handle and couldn't turn it, then began whimpering.

Maggie lay on Gretchen's bed in a haze of resentment. Now she was going to have to tend to Stevie!

Polly, on the other side of the door, was already doing so. Maggie heard her as she carried Stevie away again. In a moment she heard Stevie giggling. Polly switched on the TV. Maggie put her head under a pillow, and hid from her life.

"Sometimes they're just too much." As soon as Maggie settled onto Rachel's wonderful stuffed chair, the tears sprang from her eyes and her throat was choked. At least Rachel would understand. She had two kids, too, Mason, who was Jay's age, and Leah, who was four. Suddenly there were a thousand things Maggie wanted to say. She wanted to tell Rachel how bad the week was going—and it was only Tuesday! She wanted to ask her what she did when Mason was sassy and sour and sad. She wanted to ask if Leah had outgrown that terrible baby neediness yet.

Rachel put her palm against her own chest. "You have to find the place—in here—where you are the truest you. You have to protect it. Children—oh, they need you, of course they do, and you want to give them what they need, but if you aren't nurturing your *self*, what kind of mother can you be, anyway? If you are an artist and you put away your paints? A writer and you close the drawer on your manuscript? Children need parents who are whole and authentic."

Maggie didn't think she and Rachel were talking about the same things at all.

"Of course you don't write," Rachel said.

"Or paint." Maggie smiled, thinking it was better if she made light of her lack of talent.

Rachel settled onto a chaise lounge across from Maggie. "Once you have a child, everyone sees you as part of a unit. I had to change therapists two times to get away from the family systems bias. Kids or not, I want to be an individual. My work doesn't have anything to do with the kids. The writing, I mean." She crossed her legs and settled down deeper in the cushions. "I'm thinking about taking a leave from teaching. We don't really need the money. I've hit a plateau with this manuscript. There's something deeper evading me, and I don't think I can dig down to it when I have so many distractions. Actually, it may not be a matter of digging. It may be a matter of soaring, of finding the overarching theme, the ultimate story. You know what I mean?"

Maggie nodded yes, but she felt dizzy with bafflement. She also felt intimidated. It was Rachel who had asked her to join their splinter group when the larger book group broke up. Right away it was obvious she wasn't as well-read, as knowledgeable as Nora or Rachel, but neither was Gretchen (whom Maggie had immediately suggested), and they were never unkind. Rachel was in some way the group's spirit: she chided them to probe inside, to think harder, to relate everything, ultimately, to the deepest part of themselves. Maggie often felt a mistiness in her own thinking, as if Rachel's concepts were just out of reach, obscured, but attainable, if she made the effort. She had always felt she should try.

Rachel gazed beyond Maggie, at the wall behind, where there were a dozen or more photographs of herself at various ages. "When I began this novel, I thought it was a journey story. Daphne moves out from the house—at night, I told you this before, didn't I—in circles, widening the territory, exploring the night of her neighborhood, her town, even as she is exploring her own dark side—and the circles widen, and I thought, well, eventually she'll go out far enough that she won't come back. She'll be free, she'll be somewhere she hasn't been before. Then I realized there had to be something more objective than that, something tangible, a desire, and I embodied that in the Other—you don't know if it's a man or a woman. But you know what I've discovered?" She sat up, her shoulders now raised, her head bent toward Maggie. "That intensity of desire, once abated, creates stasis. It's anticlimactic." She fell back on the chair again. "It's boring." She lifted her hands, palms up, and smiled ruefully. "Maybe it's inevitable. Maybe fulfillment means closure, and closure is—for me at least—*dishwater.*"

There was a timid knock at the door, the door squeaked open slightly, and Leah peeked around. "Mommy, we're having rice pudding."

"I'm so sorry," Rachel said, looking at Maggie. To Leah, she spoke sternly. "I'm talking now."

"But Daddy said to tell you."

"Tell Daddy I'm busy."

Leah's face clouded. She inched the door open a bit wider, put one foot inside the room.

"You may not come in now," Rachel said.

Maggie jumped up. "I need to go anyway. The kids need baths, stories—" She lifted her hands the same way Rachel had done earlier, palms up.

Leah ran across the room and stood by her mother.

"You set boundaries," Rachel said. Maggie nodded mutely.

"And you separate issues, those that have to do with—them—" she glanced at her daughter—"and those that have to do with you."

"I better go." Maggie's face burned. Leah looked like a child mannequin, standing by her mother, a pretty child with no expression at all just now.

Rachel heaved herself off the chair. Leah clung to her long pink dress. Rachel moved across to Maggie and put her arm over her shoulder. "A therapist could help you sort it out, you know," she said. "The right one."

Maggie took a breath and found a voice. "I was really just wondering what you do when Mason—when he—sometimes he must—"

Rachel smiled. "Sandy looks after the kids in the evenings, so I can work. I really leave the discipline—that's what you're asking about, isn't it?—to him. You could talk to him." She kissed Maggie's cheek. Leah had followed her movement across the room. She stood pressed against her hip, her face still blank and patient.

"Bye, Leah," Maggie said.

Rachel glanced down as if she'd only just noticed the child. She patted her shoulder. "Run have your dessert, angel." To Maggie she said, "Come any time."

Maggie took Leah's hand. By the time they were at the stairs, she heard Rachel's door close firmly with a click.

* * *

Dulce tells me: Rachel was one of the first people I met when I moved to Lupine. Gus was four-and-a-half. I had to find work, but I didn't know what I could do so that I could also afford a babysitter. I had a place to live, and I applied for food stamps, but I didn't want to go to welfare. My husband was in prison. I didn't want nobody asking me questions. I didn't want to answer to nobody.

There was an ad in the paper for a babysitter, "Live in or out." I went and talked to her. I saw that what she really wanted was a housekeeper, cook, laundress, and *babysitter, so I promised her I could do everything, if she would hire me, and if I could keep Gus with me whenever I was in her house. Her son Mason was the same age as Gus, so it made it easier for me, and was good for the boys. Rachel was teaching, and she was soon pregnant with Leah. I didn't know what her husband Sandy did, exactly, because he was in and out all the time, but that was his business and I never thought about it. I knew it had to do with money. I guess I thought he was a banker, except that he didn't seem to have a schedule. Now I know he's just rich. He goes somewhere when he feels like it, and he plays with his own money. And, you suppose, he makes more of it. He's nice, Sandy. He was always good to Gus. He never really could decide how to act around me, though. Americans don't know how to act with servants. My papa told me once that in Mexico, everyone has someone who helps out in the house, except the poor campesinos. Everyone understands, you aren't friends. Sandy always wanted me to know how much he appreciated what I did. He could have given me more money and I could have done my own things with my son, but he didn't pay me, Rachel did.*

Well, little by little I moved some clothes over to their house and spent most weekday nights there, then went home to our trailer on the weekends. That was what made me finally like the trailer. I had hated it at first, because of the way I got it, and where it was. I liked the way it was mine, we had our privacy, but it was cozy, tucked in so close to the other trailers. I liked not doing nothing for other people, being the lady of my own shitty little house.

I admired Rachel, but she was frightening in some ways. For one thing, she was very large, a tall, big-boned woman, with a belly that looked ready to burst with triplets, at least. She was intense, and nosy, and full of advice. She insisted on taking Gus to Mason's pediatrician. She thought he ought to be growing faster; her son was much bigger. I told her, my papa was a short man. I'm only 5'2''. I didn't say anything about Gus' father, and Rachel didn't ask. She gave me Mason's old clothes for Gus. When I went home on Friday she sent me with a sack of groceries, leftover roast, and fruit, bags of potatoes. I worked long hours; it really was like being the wife and mother of a large family, but I was happy that the boys got along so well. And I didn't have to worry too much, since we ate ten or twelve meals a week at their place. We ate like family. Most of the time, it was Sandy and me and the kids. Sandy said Rachel ate in the middle of the night. She was getting strange. He told me he appreciated the way I looked after the kids. Often in the afternoon I took them to the park and sat on a folded blanket and watched them play, and felt lucky. I wanted to write Gustavo and say we were okay, but I felt guilty; I thought things ought to be worse for a woman whose husband was in prison. As long as I didn't look back and I didn't look too far forward, I felt almost happy. I could watch my son grow. I could figure out something more at another time.

After Leah was born, the load on me was much heavier. Rachel stayed in bed for weeks, all the time she had off from school. She didn't nurse Leah. She slept a lot in the day. She wanted me to keep the kids quiet. She got up at night and wandered around downstairs, sometimes until morning. I began to feel the tension between her and Sandy, too, but it wasn't my place to say nothing, and what would I have said? I went to the health food store and bought herbs to calm her. She laughed. When she saw she'd insulted me, she said she'd try them, but that was the last I heard. My papa's grandmother was a healer. Even my mother knows herbs. She buys them in fancy sealed bottles at the supermarket.

The boys began going to kindergarten. We enrolled them in the afternoon session in Mason's neighborhood so that there wouldn't be any hurry in the morning. I could put Leah down for her nap part of the time they were gone. At first I slept then, too, but after a while I began to think of the time as mine, and I didn't want to waste it. That was when I began a dream book. I used one of those little school notebooks.

Some dreams I had over and over again—the children in the orange grove, for example, and the girl on the balcony. Others I had only once, and I was anxious to write them down. I often wrote in Spanish, though I had never really studied or read it. Writing kept the language in my head. Besides, I dreamt in Spanish, most of the time.

In May of that year, the year the boys were in kindergarten, Rachel told me that she would "take over" the care of Leah in the summer. For certain, I said. To myself, I thought: well, why shouldn't you, you're the mother! But she hadn't ever taken care of Leah. I was sure that when I did not stay in the house, it was Sandy who got up with Leah. Even if Rachel was up, reading, or walking, or, eventually, writing, she would ignore her daughter's cries. I don't mean she was cruel. I think she didn't hear. Me, I dream when I'm asleep. Rachel dreams, walking around.

So there won't be so much for you to do, she said. She thought maybe I could come just in the mornings. Well, that would cut my pay in half, wouldn't it? But I didn't say anything right away; I needed to go home and think about it, think about what else I could do. Then she said she'd also been thinking she wanted to concentrate on her writing more, and she thought she needed a quieter house, and would I please not bring Gus anymore? Like he was a puppy.

What did she think I was going to do with him in the summer? She was paying me less than minimum wage, and now that was for only half a day, and did she think I could find a babysitter who would charge me even less? Did she think I would have anything left over?

I went to welfare. I cried for days before I did it, but I didn't see what else I could do. When I went in, I had this feeling, like they'd known all along I'd be in. Like maybe my mother had called ahead! Well, I told them I would work if they would pay for child care, but that's not how it goes. All that summer I was home with him, and I should have been happy, I should have enjoyed it—and I did, much of the time, especially when we were outside—but I was frantic to find work and a way to live. I told Rachel I would come once a week to clean, but I had to bring Gus. She said it wasn't possible. She found someone else, a service, to do the cleaning. You can bet she paid them more than she'd ever paid me. I heard that they come in, two of them, and it's $25 an hour. They're fast. But if I'm slower, I'm cheaper, and I was there, why wasn't that as good?

In the fall, when Gus started first grade, I began working as a dishwasher. I worked a lunch shift in a restaurant that did its biggest business then. The next year I began working in a motel part-time, and they taught me how to speed up. Oh, and Rachel asked me if I would come back. She wanted me twice a week. She gave me more money. She said the other people she had hired hadn't cared about the house, about her things, and she had to tell them every thing to do, she had to make lists, couldn't they see what was in front of their eyes?

One day she said, I suppose Gus could come over here after school if you're not done. He was in second grade, and he was going home to the trailer alone after school when I had work. I said I had made other arrangements. Once, after that, Sandy took both boys up to Portland to a comic book convention, if you can imagine that, and to the science museum. I know it was nice of him, but afterwards, when Gus said he wanted to call Mason, I'd say, wait for them to call you, and they didn't. It hurt his feelings a lot. Then he started being friends with your little Jay, and that was a lot better. They both loved comic books and soccer and school, and it was nice, because of them being in the same classroom. And Jay little, like Gus, except Gus is stocky.

Rachel recommended me to other people. First to her mother-in-law, who was a lot more formal and direct, and nice but not friendly. Also I worked sometimes for Nora, then later, Nora sent me to Lynn, and there were some others.

Last summer Rachel invited us—Gus and me—to a barbecue at her house on July 4th. She said it would just be family. I was uneasy; family would include Sandy's mother, who was always politely cool to me. I didn't want to go, but Gus did, and I didn't know how to refuse. Gus wasn't in the same school as Mason anymore, and he wanted to see him.

It turned out there was a lot of family—Sandy's sister and her husband and kids, the grandparents, and another couple and their kids were "god-kin" someone told me. I was com-

pletely out of place, crazy to go, but Gus liked being with the kids. Everyone was there in shorts and those tube tops and jerseys, except Sandy's mother, who wore a white pants outfit, and me, in a dress, looking like I'd gone to some other event.

Everyone helped Rachel get the food out. We sat in the yard around tables. Someone asked me if I was a neighbor. I was surprised Sandy's mother hadn't told them who I was, but maybe she didn't know I was coming. I said I lived across town, near the bowling alley, and I'd worked for Rachel for several years. Rachel said, Oh my yes, what would I have done without her? She's been with me since before Leah was born. I could see them wondering what else they could possibly ask me. And I was thinking about that phrase, being "with" someone. The only person I'd ever been "with" was Gustavo. Rachel had never asked me, not once, about Gus' father. She probably thought I wasn't married. So there we are at a picnic, drinking lemonade and eating strawberries and eggcake, and I'm going over all this stuff in my head, over and over until my skull feels like it's splitting. Then, when the meal was over, and everyone was moaning about how delicious it had been—there wasn't much of anything I liked, truthfully, it was all very bland—Rachel asked me if I'd mind clearing the table. Nobody else even looked my way when she asked. Nobody paid the slightest bit of attention when I took the mess away. Nobody peeked in as I covered dishes of leftovers and scraped the plates and loaded the dishwasher and scrubbed the stove. Nobody admired how fast I worked.

I sat in the kitchen and waited for Gus to come in the house for something. He and Mason and one other boy were going to put on a video. I grabbed him and said we were going. He didn't protest a bit; he's always been very sensitive that way. We left without saying goodbye.

Lynn's house was bleached wood, cool glass and stainless steel. She displayed a hat that had belonged to a famous movie star (Dorothy Lamour?), a huge papier mâché pig, a collection of thimbles. She always had fresh flowers—from her garden, in season, from the florist's, other times—and magazines and large expensive books on the tables. She disliked things out of place. Only one room was disorderly, the room where her husband Dermott wrote; in there, Dulce vacuumed and carried away dirty dishes, leaving a desk, bed, the carpet strewn with papers and books. The house was beautiful, in its way, but odd for people to live in. Lynn always walked barefoot—she had Chinese slippers for her friends when they came—and dressed simply, in expensive stretchy one-piece things, with something thrown over to flow—a scarf, a silky vest, a sarong.

Dulce was on her hands and knees in the master bathroom. Lynn had dropped a bottle of something sticky, maybe days ago, and it was hard to get up, especially since Lynn wanted no strong cleansers—she gave Dulce a citrus concentrate to use for everything. Through the open door Dulce heard Lynn and Dermott talking. Dermott wanted her to go with him to play tennis, she said she didn't have time. He said why didn't she buy a tray at Safeway's—cheese and cut-up veggies, a tray of fancy crackers? Lynn said, "The way I see it, you left L.A. to get away from meetings and traffic and high-calorie lunches, but we still have to have a home. We still have people popping in from L.A. like it was a bus stop away, and they matter, this is your work, Dermott, a writer has to pay attention to these things. This is not exactly back to nature. Lupine has its standards; we have ours. You can wear cut-off sweats and run out for a six-pack of beer, but cheese and crackers on a paper plate are low-class. What will your Hollywood cronies think of Muenster and Wheat Thins? What will they pay you for a script? 'He lives in Or-y-gone,' they'll say. 'And Lynn has gone to hell.'"

Dulce scraped up strips of goo and threw them in the toilet. She straightened a moment and stretched to ease her back.

Dermott said, "You don't have any of those worries tonight, Lynn, we're having friends over. Lighten up." Dulce heard him kissing, making smacking noises; Lynn make pipping sounds. "I hope you're not tired when I get home," he said. "I hope the house is clean and the bed is made." There was a smacking sound. "To your satisfaction."

Dulce flushed the toilet.

When she got to the kitchen, Lynn was sitting in the breakfast alcove (that was what she called it) drinking a glass of white wine and nibbling at small chunks of cantaloupe off a patterned ceramic dish. She glanced up as Dulce arrived. "Sometimes I sit here in the dark. The raccoons come down and wrestle on the deck. Do you have raccoons where you live?"

"No. Only cats and skunks." Actually, Dulce had opened her door last night, to get more air, and caught a glimpse of two baby raccoons staring at her from the center of the drive through the court. She didn't see why Lynn would want to discuss animals with her, though, or anything else.

Lynn twirled her glass between her palms. "We had a house in the canyon outside L.A. Once I saw a wild cat frisking in the brush like a kitten. I heard coyotes at night. I lost a toy terrier to one. Sounds awful, but I miss all that."

"You must have birds, squirrels, here," Dulce said. She held Lynn's list in her hand. She was supposed to clean the refrigerator this time. "Should I do the kitchen later?"

Lynn's fingers fluttered. "No, no. I'll do my Nordic Track and wash my hair." She drained her glass. "Have a little lunch if you want. Try my hors d'ouevres. Mushroom caps stuffed with boursin and spinach." She smiled. "A hell of a lot of trouble."

Dulce snapped a towel and laid it in the sink. She began putting bottles and jars from the refrigerator there, to stay cool while she cleaned. Behind her, Lynn padded away.

When Dulce reached the bedroom, she found the bed piled with clothes. Lynn sat at her mirror, examining her face. "What do you think, Dulce? I'm thirty-six. Four more good years? Five?" She was wearing a wine-colored body suit. She was so thin her clavicles protruded. Her pale hair was wet and combed slick back from her face. She looked young and a little sick, though Dulce knew she was athletic, ate all the right things, went to doctors and dentists in L.A.

"What should we do with these?" Dulce surveyed the amazing, enormous mound of clothes. There seemed to be something of everything, skirts and dresses, pants, sweaters, jackets.

"I went crazy this morning," Lynn said. She rose and reached into her closet for a pale silky short robe. "I'm never going to wear any of that. Not here. Not anywhere. There's something—well, immoral—about so many things stuffed into your closet." She threw open the doors and pointed into the closet. "Besides, now you can clean the inside really well. Up along those ridges—" She reached in and tapped the closet wall. "I hate thinking of all that dust."

Dulce had begun to fold and stack clothes on the floor. Lynn watched her a moment, then spoke. "Isn't there anything you can use? Take anything." She stepped over next to Dulce and dug into the pile, came up with a red sweater. "This is cashmere, feel. It's pretty, but I look like a whore in it. My blond hair—" She held it up to Dulce. "With your dark coloring, it'd be smashing."

The clothes, Dulce guessed, were fours and sixes. The sweater looked like a child's. All the items were wool or silk or fine cotton. Dulce wondered what they had cost, totalled, what a person could do with the money this abundance represented.

She tried to smile. "I'm four inches shorter than you, Lynn, and who knows how much bigger around."

Lynn threw a skirt onto the floor, dug down for a jacket, held it up in the air. "This is one of those shapeless, sizeless styles, you could wear it—"

"No thank you," Dulce said firmly. She began, again, to fold.

Lynn hurried away, and returned with a box of lawn

bags. She thrust them at Dulce. "Here, put everything in bags. I'll call Goodwill to pick up. And then strip the bed. Everything. I've bought new covers for the mattress and pillows, my allergies, you know. Something the dust mites can't get through." It was obvious she was annoyed with Dulce.

"Yes ma'am," Dulce said.

Lynn stopped her silly, frantic motion, and stared. "You're in your socks," she said.

Dulce stuffed sweaters into one of the bags. "I didn't want to track anything in," she said. The plastic bag made a lot of noise. Whatever Lynn said was lost.

Across town, Maggie has retreated to her cottage with her children, while Polly settles the new baby. Jay is home another day, miserable, with raw patches of poison oak on his neck and both cheeks. Maggie wouldn't dream of saying "I told you so." (She didn't even think of poison oak.) Besides, this way he avoids the last-minute Spanish night rehearsals from which he is excluded.

She has put him in her bed, with extra pillows from Polly's, a plastic jug of ice water, a pile of comic books. He moans and whimpers, milking his condition, and Maggie tries to give him all the sympathy he seems to require. She takes his temperature and gives him Tylenol. She puts ointment on his sore places. She suggests he call his father and tell him what has happened, but when they try the cycle shop in Austin, they find he is out. Disappointed, Jay pouts. Maggie takes Stevie for a long walk, on which they encounter a puppy in a neighbor's yard, and are invited to play. For a little while, time passes pleasantly.

By the time they return, they are all hungry. They have been eating so much at Polly's, Maggie hasn't been to the grocery store in days. She mixes canned tuna with mayonnaise, and digs out crackers and a jar of juice. Stevie plays with the food and gets part of it in her mouth. Jay complains and whines for a hamburger. Maggie reminds him that his dad will be calling, and he might miss him if they go out. Jay glumly eats a small lump of tuna and retreats again to Maggie's bed.

Stevie toddles to her book basket and retrieves *Runaway Bunny.* Maggie is pleased to stretch out on the couch with her and read it. As she turns each page, Stevie shrieks with delighted recognition, slaps the picture, and calls out "Bunny!" (or her approximation). She likes for Maggie to read the same lines again and again. Maggie doesn't mind. In fact, she loves the book. No matter where the bunny runs away, the mother finds him. It is Maggie's favorite children's story.

The phone rings, and before she can shift Stevie from her lap, Jay has leapt and run to answer. "Dad?" he says, instead of hello, and then his face clouds and he hands the phone to Maggie and runs back to bed.

It is Lynn. "I've been going through my closets. I have this heap of clothes, they're all fine, you know I just keep changing my mind about what I want. I was wondering if you'd want to come over and take a look, I think there are things you could teach in." She talks so fast, Maggie is a beat behind her, understanding.

"I can't, Lynn, I've got the kids. Jay's got poison oak."

"Couldn't Polly watch them?"

"She's got a new foster child, I didn't tell you? A baby, six weeks. She just came today."

"So what about this stuff? Should I hold onto it until you can get over?"

"Lynn, the school year's over, I haven't got a job, believe me, the few things I have are enough for my life. I just can't see myself in your clothes."

"You're little enough."

"And you're nice to offer, but I don't think so."

There is a long pause, then Lynn says, "I ought to take all this stuff back to L.A. to one of those resale shops. It's all like new. I can't believe I can't give it away."

Stevie rubs her eyes and clings to Maggie's hip.

"It's the kids—I can't talk—" she says.

Lynn says, "Listen, I have this idea. I have a massage appointment at two. It's just half an hour. Why don't you take it, my treat? It sounds like something you really need." That said with conviction, she adds, more tentatively, "I guess I could watch the kids that long."

Maggie has always thought Lynn is the prettiest, cleverest woman she knows. She admires her for a hundred things. Right now, though, she wonders if Lynn is speaking to her from another planet. "I've got to go," she says. "Believe me, you don't want to trade your massage for my kids."

Lynn laughs. "I'll get you a certificate. You can go when you have time. Really, it takes away all the tension. It dissolves it. It's so good for you."

"Let me think about it, Lynn. I've got to go."

"Okay. See you Saturday."

"What?"

"Nora's lunch."

"Right. Bye."

She hangs up and pulls Stevie close against her, between her body and the back of the couch. Stevie is already dozing. She also smells dirty. "Oh baby girl, I'm tired of diapers," Maggie whispers. With enormous effort, she changes Stevie, who fusses halfheartedly and falls back asleep.

Mo calls shortly after. Maggie tells him about Jay's poison oak. She tells him about Polly's baby, who is tiny and fragile and red with anger. She tells him about Lynn's offer to send her for a massage.

"I could do that for free," he says.

Oh, she would like that, she thinks, longing flushing over her body. "If you were here," she says.

"If you were here," he says.

"You better talk to Jay." She puts the phone down and wakes Jay.

Sleepily, Jay tells his dad about the shed and the poison oak. "Are you going to come?" he asks.

He hands the phone to Maggie. "He wants you."

Mo wants to know when school is out. It's only a couple of weeks. "We'll figure something out soon," he says. "I've got to go."

Jay is watching her. "What'd he say? Is he coming?"

"Some time."

He turns on his heel, and this time he slams the door to her bedroom.

They need to talk about their son, she thinks. She and Mo. They really do need to talk.

Dulce sat to one side near the back of the gym to watch the skits on Spanish night. She thought that what the kids were enjoying—and they *were* having a good time—was the fun of dressing up and acting silly. Spanish had very little to do with it. There were jumping beans and big bad wolves, señoritas with huge paper fans, a funny game of futbol. There were songs and poems and jumprope rhymes. Through it all, even as she enjoyed the children's enthusiasm, Dulce couldn't help wondering who all this Spanish was for. Would these children travel to Mexico, to Costa Rica, to Spain? Would they find jobs someday where they needed Spanish to talk to their uneducated clients? (Social workers, policemen?) Did they know anybody who actually spoke Spanish? Did they want to?

The parents had brought food. There was an intermission, and everyone attacked the many pots of salsa and bowls of chips, beans and tortillas, mounds of red rice. She had made a tray of sliced French bread sweetened with dark brown sugar and cinnamon, a treat she remembered from childhood. No one spoke to her. She stood against the wall with a wedge of her own food in her hand, alone until Gus made his way to her. He was eating a tortilla spread with avocado.

"Nobody's going to like that stuff," he said, pointing to his mother's bread. Then she couldn't help watching, as people looked over the food, and neglected the *pan*. "I'm the main bad wolf," her son said. His brown cheeks were rosy with excitement. "Can you see me from back there?"

At the end of the skits, awards were presented. It was so hot in the gym, and the show had gone on so long, Dulce was half-asleep when she heard her son's name. *Gus Quirarte.* She opened her eyes. She leaned forward to watch him walk up to the stage from his place with his class down below. Was this something he had competed for? His expression was one of delight, and surprise: I won something! it said. But what? He was awarded the Language Camp Scholarship. There was much applause. He descended the steps, clutching a certificate, and scanned the audience, looking for his mother. She waved quickly, just above her head. Later he said he wasn't sure what it was for. Learning Spanish, that was all he knew. He liked that. He liked Spanish. He had learned a lot from Lupe's family, from Hilario. "The teacher said it comes to me naturally," he said. He smiled a smart-aleck smile.

Thursday she cleaned eleven rooms at the motel, then drove home slowly. The car was making strange noises. She said *Jesus, Mary, Joseph* over and over even though she knew she was silly. She changed and went over to the school as the kids were being dismissed. Mrs. Cecil wasn't in the office. The secretary said she was somewhere in the building, and paged her. Dulce sat on the chair by the principal's door. She didn't cross her legs. She folded her hands in her lap, and sat up straight. She wondered how many more times, good or bad, she would have to come to her son's school. She wondered if she would ever stop feeling out of place.

Across the hall, Maggie is in conference with Jennifer, the counselor. Earlier in the afternoon, she was summoned to school to collect Jay and take him home. He had excused himself from class to go to the bathroom, then had gone outside and let the air out of nine bicycles before someone happened to notice him down on his knees busy with mischief.

Now, as requested, she has returned to talk. Jay, deeply sullen, has hidden himself in his dad's old room and refused this very thing, talk. Polly has been oddly silent, offering little comfort and no advice, though she says she's making spaghetti, and could Maggie pick up French bread? Maggie left Stevie peering into the baby's crib while Polly held her hand and explained the baby was resting. She felt extra, not quite necessary. It was somehow her fault that things were going wrong for Jay. As if accused, she felt hot with resentment.

Jennifer says she wonders if there is some particular impulse for Jay's behavior. Maggie considers the word, impulse. It does seem relevant. Mo's impulse to flee. Polly's impulse to mother. Jay's impulse to *be trouble.* Maggie's own lack of impulse. She knows what she does not want to do—does not want to leave Lupine, does not want to be without Mo, does not want to talk to Jennifer, does not want to take hand-me-downs or advice from her friends. It is a humiliating word for Maggie, impulse. It suggests energy, rhythm, getting-off-the-dime. Maybe Jay's impulse is to get his mother moving? Maybe Jay's impulse is to demand that *something be done?* But what?

Maggie knows that this woman Jennifer means well. She is a little older than Maggie, maybe thirty-two or -three, a soft-spoken but efficient professional, with notes and brightly colored files in a plastic stand behind her. She has already added up a few things: Jay's declining performance in school, the acceleration of his bad moods, his withdrawal from his friends.

"I'm not sure that's true," Maggie interrupts Jennifer's monologue. "The part about his friends. I think he feels they've deserted him. Gus, at least. They've played together the last couple of years. Now Gus is busy—this new boy—" She thinks Jennifer would be full of advice, if only Maggie told her how things are, but Maggie doesn't think Jennifer can understand. How simple it would be to say, Jay's angry because he got left out last night. He's hurt because his best friend is otherwise occupied. He's lonesome for his dad, and hey, he hasn't even been able to buy the high-top athletic shoes he's wanted for months.

"Maybe Jay and I can repair the bicycles," Maggie says. She has never pumped a tire, but surely she can learn fast enough.

"Don't worry. One of the teachers and a couple of sixth graders took care of it. There was no harm done, really. He just unscrewed the caps and pushed the plungers—"

"He's never done anything like this before." Maggie feels helpless and accused. She wishes Jay had thought about what he was doing, what it would mean for her. Of course he probably did think. He thought: *I hate them all.* Or: *Take that.*

"I want to show you something," Jennifer says. She turns and takes a piece of paper from one of the files behind her. It is a drawing. She hands it to Maggie. "I was in Jay's class last week. Sometimes I do little exercises. I try to give them a chance to talk about their feelings. This time, I asked them to draw their houses. You see what he's done."

Maggie, whose vision is perfect, holds the crayoned drawing in front of her face as if it is a difficult puzzle, so that Jennifer is talking to the back of it, unable to see either Maggie or the picture.

There is Polly's red house, and garage, and behind, the cottage. "My house," Jay has labeled the cottage. Beside the garage he has drawn something, then scribbled it out with black crayon.

"I asked him about the marked-out part," Jennifer says.

Maggie lays the drawing on her lap and lets Jennifer tell her what she has already figured out. "It's his dad's truck. He says that's where he always parks it when he's home."

"What do you want me to tell you?" Maggie says quietly. "If you've figured everything out?"

Jennifer blushes. "I didn't mean to imply—"

"A little boy is hurt and confused. He's a child. Why did his teacher throw him out of Spanish night? What did he learn from that?" She stands up. "I'll take this," she says, shaking the drawing slightly, "back to Jay." She is thinking maybe he should send it to Mo, but she doesn't say that now, to Jennifer.

"Maggie—" Jennifer is on her feet. She reaches out,

but stops before she actually touches Maggie. Maggie's hand trembles visibly. She puts her arm down alongside her thigh.

"I need to ask your permission—your advice—" Jennifer does touch Maggie, gently, on her elbow, but only for a moment.

"Permission for what?"

"There are still two weeks. We have groups. Jay. He could share his feelings. He could find out how other kids are feeling about these same issues. I think it would help."

"I beg your pardon?"

"It's a question of which group. The anger group, or the loss group? The anger group would help him get a handle for now, but the other—I think he might do better with those children—"

"I'll have to think about it." Maggie backs toward the door. "I'll talk to his dad. I'll talk to Jay."

Outside, she makes it to the corner of the building before she begins to cry. She stops, leans against the brick wall, thinks of other things she might have said. She wishes Polly had come. She wishes Jay had not messed with the bikes.

"Are you okay?"

She jumps. She wipes her eyes with the back of her hand. At first, she doesn't know who is there, then she realizes it is Gus' mother. Dulce.

"Are you sick?"

"No. Upset." She tries to smile. "Called to school, you know."

"Yeah. It makes me nervous to come. It made me nervous, every day I ever went to school."

"I'm okay. Thanks." She points to the parking lot. "My car's over there. Are you going that way?"

"No. I'm walking."

"Want a ride?"

"That's okay."

"No. Really. Let me give you a ride, Dulce. Listen, would you want—could we get a cup of coffee or something? I just have a little time, but—well, would you?"

They go to the Coffee Bliss. It looks as if half the town has picked now to take a break. There's no place to sit. Dulce says, "I just live behind, in the trailer court. Why don't we go there? You've never been to my place. It'll be quiet. Gus won't be home yet." She looks around.

"Let me get our coffee," Maggie says, but when Dulce lays two quarters on the counter, she doesn't object. She would like to pay; she is never the one to pay. Polly pays. Her friends pay. She would like to pay, but maybe Dulce, like her, never pays. Maybe it's better to bear one's own cost.

The first thing that strikes her, once they are inside Dulce's trailer, is how much like the cottage it is. The compact kitchen, the slightly shabby couch, obviously used as a bed—a pillow and blanket are piled at one end—and the sense of efficiency, of fitting in the space you happen to have.

Drawings are scotch-taped to the walls. "Gus'?" she says, touching one. A knight on a horse leans over to slash with his sword at a scaly monster.

"He's always at it." Dulce arranges chairs for them at her small table. They pull the caps off their coffee cups and drink. Maggie feels shy, but comfortable, too. It doesn't seem necessary to find something to say right away.

Near the edge of the table is a stack of more drawings. Idly, she touches the edges, lifts the top—a moat, and trees—and sees, below it, an odd map. "It looks like Texas," she says, though she can see that the map shows castles and lakes, mountains and forests, a land of dragons.

Dulce slides the drawing along the table closer to her and studies it for a moment. "He creates these kingdoms," she says. "He reads fantasies. Or used to. He hasn't been doing it so much lately." She places the paper back on the stack, face down.

"Is it just the two of you?" Maggie asks. She is slightly embarrassed. Jay has talked about Gus for a couple of years, has been to his home, swapped comic books, but Maggie has, at most, spoken to Dulce a few times on the phone, said hello at school events, passed her without attention at Rachel's, and never had the slightest curiosity about her. Yet she has extraordinary looks: amazing hair and eyes, a voluptuousness that she seems to take matter-of-factly, and a way of regarding you, a gaze, that calms and invites confidence, without giving anything away.

Dulce nods, looking away slightly. "For a long time," she says. She gestures toward the upside-down drawing. "That's where his father is now. Texas. The map. I guess he's thinking about his dad."

"Oh!" Maggie exclaims. A chill runs down her neck. "That's so strange!"

Dulce regards her passively, but Maggie rushes to explain. "Because that's where Mo is, too. Jay's father." Dulce gives the slightest nod, asks nothing, and sips her coffee, but Maggie rushes on as if commanded to give details. "He has a friend there, from the army. He has this job—" On and on she goes, like a toy wound tight, talking and talking, as Dulce calmly finishes her coffee. "Jay is so upset." She recounts his recent misadventures. "I don't know what I should do. Maybe Mo will come up to get him. I didn't want to go to Texas. I don't think I want to go—I don't know what I should do—"

She hears herself babbling. "Do you know what time it is?"

Dulce turns around to read a little clock on the stove. "A quarter to five," she says.

"Oh no, I've got to go. My mother-in-law—there's this other baby—"

Dulce gets up with her. "Texas is not the end of the world, is it?"

"But it has dragons, remember?" She has a fierce urge to hug Dulce. Then she thinks: "You never said why you were at school. Was Gus in trouble, too?"

"They want to send my son to the college for three weeks to study Spanish," Dulce says. "They want him to be Mexican." For some reason, that makes her laugh. "I might as well send him to Texas, too."

"Oh Maggie!" Polly says. She looks more frazzled than Maggie can ever remember seeing her since Mo's father died. Stevie is on the living room floor, nested in an enormous pile of toys and pots, bowls and books. The baby, in the hall crib, cries in shrill bursts, stopping to gulp, whimper, then explode again. "All I asked you to do was pick up a loaf of bread!" Maggie turns and runs to the car. When she comes back with milk and bread and a quart of strawberries, Polly is draining spaghetti, and Jay is setting the table. Stevie is in her high chair, chewing on a chunk of cheese. The baby is asleep. Maggie has decided that the best thing is to pretend that nothing is wrong. She doesn't know what else to do.

Polly empties the spaghetti into a dish and comes to put her arm around Maggie. "I'm sorry I yelled at you," she says. Maggie squeezes her waist. The bad moment is gone, but the baby is not. Polly had to know this would happen, but it didn't keep her from taking the baby.

Polly turns the TV so she can watch the news as they eat. Jay moves his spaghetti around with his fork and steals glances at Maggie. Maggie makes much of helping Stevie with her messy meal. Then she takes her children to their own beds in the cottage, opens a book she is too sleepy to read, and waits for Mo to call.

"What do you think?" she asks him when she has explained about the counseling groups.

"I think I should come soon. They mean well, but we need to solve our own problems."

"I wish we were in a book with a really good ending."

She's glad he doesn't make fun of her.

He just says, "Maybe we are."

Dulce reads her dream book, and tells herself she will know what to do, when it's time.

Gus is working on his map. He has to know she can see it, see that it is Texas, so he probably expects her to say something, but unless she's angry, she is a person who holds her opinion close and waits until she knows the best thing to say. She washes and dresses for bed. "Don't stay up too late," she tells her son. He tells her good night and raises his face to her kiss.

She has an idea. "What will you be doing Saturday?"

He shrugs. "Hanging out."

"With Hilario?"

"Sure."

"Could you ask your friend Jay along? Is there any reason you couldn't do that?"

Gus shakes his head, but it isn't really an answer. "He's really weird lately," he says. He considers the matter a moment longer. "Sure, okay."

He waits until she is in her room to say one more thing. "I'm going to write Dad."

She nods, even though he can't see her. "You should," she says. And so should I.

* * *

Dulce says she dreams tales she knows her father told her when she was a small child. Like the chicken party.

The boy's grandmother tells him to kill a chicken for dinner. He creeps out to the yard in front of their house where the chickens scratch in the dirt. All over the yard he runs, until he is tired and excited, until the chickens, too, are tired, until they run together in a huddle like turkeys and make a mound, their black chicken eyes fixed on him. He has never killed a chicken, but he has watched his abuela and his mama, and he knows he must wring the neck. From inside the open door of the small house, his grandmother calls out, Salvador, bring me the chicken. He reaches into the mound, and the world blurs with flying feathers. The air fills with the sounds of squawks and flapping, and when he is done, he has killed eight chickens.

Oh now his mama will say his name shamefully, and his grandmother will put him on his pallet all day and all night. He weeps over the chickens at his feet. He cries, so sorry! I feel it so much! But when the women come from the house and see what he has done, they hold their sides, laughing. They cry out, Oh no, Salvador, all the chickens? They call their neighbors on all sides, they make a feast.

Dulce says: When I wake from such a dream, I can remember my father the boy, but I cannot well remember the father of the girl Dulce. When he left, I was younger than Gus is now. He went away, back to Zacatecas, because his mother was dying. Like Hilario's father, in May; oh, now that made me remember lying on my bed in the dark, listening for his step. He went away, and he never returned. My mother never spoke of it. She's smart, and she worked hard. She learned to be a medical clerk in a hospital. She said, we speak only English now. When I was thirteen, she married a man she met at the hospital, a respiratory therapist. When I was sixteen, and she was pregnant with my sister, I met Gustavo. He had come up for the pear harvest. He had long silky hair and he said things to me in Spanish I had never heard. He said he would be my lover and best friend, my father and my brother. He said he would take me away from my Anglo stepfather's house, to my own house, and I believed him.

When I dream of Gustavo, he sings to me. When I dream of Papa, he is a boy.

Dulce heard Gus let himself out quickly. She looked at the clock. Eight-fifteen. She had no work today—no paid work—but she had promised Lupe she would take her and the babies to the Clínica in the next town. (Lupe loved the U.S. idea of the well-baby checkup.) She should wash clothes, shop, mend. She wanted to cook a special chicken dish for supper, simply because there was time. Maybe a movie. Like a holiday; after all, it was Friday. Maybe there would be time for a nap. She stretched. A nap would be so pleasant—she had to laugh—even if she was just getting up!

She fluffed her pillow and checked inside the case for the two hundred dollars Gustavo sent her. She had not decided what to do with it. Her car was falling apart, her stove had only one burner, Gus needed jeans and shoes, but the money wasn't quite real. She didn't know if she would need it more, later. She had sent him a postcard recently:

Gustavo, the money is here. I am glad you are with your family. I will write, but I need time.

She washed her face with cold water and brushed her hair with long hard strokes. All week she wore it in a long braid, but at night, and on a day like this, a day of her own, she brushed it out and felt it on her shoulders and back and around her face where the short wisps escaped. Gustavo used to run his hands over and through her hair. He used to bury his face in it and take deep draughts of its scent. He bought her shampoos that smelled of flowers. He said he loved her right away for her hair, though her hair had been bound up in a net the first time he saw her behind the counter at the cafe.

Maybe she remembered wrong. Maybe he said he loved her for her eyes, and the hair came later, when she let it down in the alley behind the cafe, when she let it fall over his face while he kissed her breasts in the brush behind the cement camp house where he lived that summer. He came into the cafe with his compadres, half a dozen hot shots from L.A. up to pick pears. She was an alien in her stepfather's house, and he was beautiful, with a bandana tied around his forehead, and the pride of who he was in his face. When the season was over, she went with him. Her mother cried, then screamed at her. You learn nothing! she said. Dulce screamed back: I'll never come here again, never! It was a long time before she understood what her mother meant, understood how hard it was for her mother to see her make the same choice she had, letting her love for a dark boy send her nowhere in a white world.

The coffee jar was empty. The empty bread sack lay crumpled on the counter—had Gus really eaten a loaf of bread in two days? She made a list: coffee, bread, peanut butter, oranges, beans, a chicken, a frozen vegetable for tonight.

She tucked the list in her skirt pocket and locked the trailer. It had rained some in the night. The ground was still damp, though not soaked, and water had puddled in the rut at the bottom of her step. She stepped over it. A neighbor's cat meowed and rubbed against her ankle. She bent to pet it. "Sorry, gatito," she said. "I have nothing for you but my pity."

A few doors up, Mrs. Alder peeked out of her trailer. She was frail and suspicious. She survived, Dulce thought, only because Meals on Wheels brought her something once a day. Dulce had tried to look in on her, but Mrs. Alder always pretended she couldn't hear, and didn't let her in. Dulce thought she was afraid someone would remove her from her pitiful home, though in all the time she had lived in the court, Dulce had seen only one visitor, a son with Portland plates on his car, and he came infrequently.

She waved at the old woman, who abruptly withdrew and slammed her door. No one else was in sight. The trailers, tucked so close together you could hand something from a window into your neighbor's bedroom, looked deserted. Of course, it was a weekday. Tenants worked or went to school.

The lot sat in a hollow, rising on one end to the busy street that ran by the college, and on the other end to the alley behind the Coffee Bliss Cafe. The trailer belonged to her. When she returned from California with Gus, her mother put them in the "guest bedroom" of her lovely Anglo house, next to her younger daughter Karen, who was a year older than Gus. We don't speak Spanish in this house, she said one morning when she came in the kitchen as Dulce gave Gus his breakfast. She said, what good will it do him? Six weeks later she gave Dulce a set of keys and said, if you have your own place, you can always manage. Dulce knew what that meant.

She had not seen her mother now in two years. The last time, she ran into her in a discount store. Dulce was buying oil for the car, and washrags; her mother was buying a computer for Karen.

When she arrived at Lupe's, she found the babies (nine months and two years old) dressed in frilly dresses, with bows in their hair. Hilario had walked the four-year-old to his Head Start class. Lupe was wearing a pink dress with a wide white belt around her ample waist. She had taken pains with her hair. The trailer, hardly bigger than Dulce's, and home to four children, was neat. Outside, at the foot of the step, Lupe had built a tiny stone grotto, and in the recess had placed a laminated holy card of the Sacred Heart, a crucifix, and a plastic statue of the Virgin of Guadalupe. As they stepped out of the trailer, she stopped to kneel and kiss the crucifix. Dulce thought Lupe would be happier in one of the two towns farther north, where there were neighborhoods of Mexican families, a Mexican grocery store, and the clinic, but fate had plopped the family down, like Dulce, in Lupine, and Lupe made do, relying on Hilario (and Gus) for errands and English, Dulce for transportation, the trailer for home base. She didn't seem to mind asking for help. She seemed to think it a practical and sociable way to live. She had come from a large extended family, and was working on one of her own; people were supposed to hold each other up. For Lupe, the family was everything, and friends were family. She was the first person besides Dulce to be close to Gus.

"What do you hear from Cipriano?" Dulce asked when they were settled in the car. Lupe was in the back with the children. She could belt only the older child, and hold the baby on her lap, but at least it wasn't in the front seat.

"His mother will die very soon," she said calmly. "Then he will return."

At the clinic, where they had to wait for an hour, she was delighted to talk with other mothers. The last time she was here, she met a woman who was a second cousin of her own godmother's daughter, in Chihuahua. It was the Virgin, she later told Dulce, reminding her that it was a small world, and they were all bound. The cheerful Spanish chatter was festive. The babies clambered over their mothers' feet, and one another. The clerks went about their business as if the office were a haven of calm. The nurse came and went, smiling and joking. She wore a red blouse with her white nurse's pants. The doctor peeked out. She was East Indian; she spoke Spanish.

Dulce excused herself and went for a walk. When she returned, Lupe, beaming, said the doctor had confirmed the good health and beauty of her children. The baby had received a booster shot, and had just calmed down from crying. Her face was still red and wet. "You are so good," Lupe said, clasping the babies. Dulce didn't know if she spoke to the children, or to her.

The car was making its ragged, clanky noises, and, as they entered Lupine, the temperature gauge moved steadily toward H. Dulce slowed to a crawl and prayed for luck, at least until she could pick up Lupe's son and get them home. She refused Lupe's offer of lunch, and Lupe's face crumpled. She knew she had hurt her feelings, but she wanted to be alone again. She wanted to be busy. She headed home, driving so slowly that other cars zipped around her. One young woman came alongside and waved her middle finger obscenely. Dulce knew it was silly to be bothered, but she was. She gripped the steering wheel so hard her palms smarted.

She parked on the street and sat a moment, trying to decide if she was going to do something about the car now. If she walked to a station and asked for help, they would treat it like an emergency; it would cost more than if she made an appointment. And she didn't feel like taking care of it now. She didn't really want to know what was wrong. It was too likely to be expensive.

Thought it was rare for her to enter the Coffee Bliss—she felt out of place among its student and leisure clientele—she decided that a cup of coffee would do her good. She had enjoyed the coffee she had with Maggie. She had enjoyed sitting at her table with a woman for a little while, though she had not known what to say to Maggie's woeful stories.

She waited her turn behind several customers. As she stepped away with her mug, she saw Rachel's husband Sandy across the room. He waved to her. She waved back, then went to the service counter for cream. When she turned around, he was right behind her. He insisted she sit at his table. In fact the room was full; if she had been paying attention, she would have taken her coffee in a paper cup. She wasn't comfortable with the idea of sitting with Sandy in the cafe. It was a long time since she had talked to him, and then there had been the children to absorb their attention. She could not now ask him the only question that came to her mind, which was, didn't he have any place he needed to be?

"The kids are growing fast," he said. She smiled. There was a long awkward silence, then Sandy told her about a soccer practice he had been to the day before. Mason, a strapping boy and a natural athlete, was a budding star. All Dulce could think to counter that was that Gus had won the language scholarship. She blushed, saying it. Sandy smiled. "He's a bright kid. I wish the boys were in the same school, I miss seeing Gus." She said that would be nice, but what really crossed her mind was that it would be nice if there was someone to talk to at school occasions. She always felt so clumsy and out of place, though she had always gone when summoned, as to parent conferences, where she was told Gus was a good student and a good boy. "Does he have friends?" she asked when he was younger. The teachers said, oh yes. Everyone likes Gus. After that, she thought it was probably a good place for him to go every day.

Sandy asked her what she thought of the new science program they piloted this year. She shrugged, too embarrassed to say she didn't know what piloting meant, and she didn't know anything about what Gus did in science. Sandy said, "Maybe the trial run was only in Mason's school. It's interesting. Last week they made cradles for eggs and threw them off the roof of the school." What could she say to that?

"Where are you off to on such a beautiful day?" Sandy had an expectant, enthusiastic look, as if she might explain her plans to go horseback riding, or to shop for a new car. She took the grocery list out of her skirt pocket. "Peanut butter, bread, milk," she read. Someone behind her pushed her forward against the table as he squeezed through a knot of customers. She leaned in, clutching her list against her chest. Their faces were close for a moment, until she was able to pull back again, flushed and awkward.

"Sit right there," he said, and took her cup with his. "House special okay?" She nodded and tucked her list back in her pocket. The cafe was uncomfortably warm. The sun poured through the windows along the wall. Intense conversations rose from tables like steam. What did all these people talk about? Did they discuss books they'd read? Lovers? Did they make plans to fill their free time?

Sandy set the cup in front of her. "I'm thinking I'll take the kids up to Portland to the new science museum. Maybe Gus would like to come along." When she didn't speak, he added, "In June, after school is out." She knew she was frustrating him, not commenting, but she didn't have anything to say. If they called Gus and invited him to go, Gus could decide, but she didn't think they would ever hear about it again.

She did not know what you could see in a science museum. Stuffed things, displays, but displays of what? She had taken a general science course in high school, but she couldn't remember anything she had learned. She couldn't call up any of the words. She would have liked to go to Portland. What would he think if she told him she had never been? Maybe he would say, oh, but you lived in L.A.! because that made him think of Malibu and Hollywood. He would not have a picture in his mind of the barrio. He would not know that weeks went by and she didn't leave the block where they lived.

"Where will you stay?" she asked.

"A motel. Out by Oswego. With a swimming pool for the kids." He was staring. "Let's just plan on it. On Gus coming with us." He considered a moment, then said, "You could come."

She took a long swallow of coffee and pushed her cup aside. "I've got to get to the store now."

He stood up, too, and took her cup with his to the busing station. He walked with her through the throng to the door. Outside, in the bright sunlight, he said, "Where are you parked?"

"There's something wrong with my car. It's running hot, it's making noises." She stepped away from him. "I'm walking."

"I'll take a look," he said. "Maybe I can do something."

"No."

"I'll give you a ride."

"It's a short walk."

"Come on," he said. "I was on my way to the store right now myself." He took her elbow. It was stupid, being steered along the walk, but she didn't want to pull away and insult him.

In the car, he said he had been talking to Mason about working in the yard this summer. "I want to take a lot of bushes out, put in some new landscaping." He kept glancing at her. What did he want her to do? "Maybe Gus could help, too. I would pay him something. A boy his age, there are things he wants."

Dulce felt hot prickles on the back of her neck. "He's going to get a paper route." It was a complete lie. When he had suggested that very thing, she had discouraged him. She didn't want him going door to door, collecting.

In the store, she moved up and down the aisles, choosing house brands, thinking ahead through the week, buying more than she had intended. She glanced around several times; he wasn't in sight. The hot irritation on her skin eased.

He was waiting for her at the exit. He reached his arms out to relieve her of one of her sacks. "I'll drop you off. And take a look at the car."

He pulled into the small lot behind the Coffee Bliss and helped her with the groceries. "They tow." She pointed to a sign on the back of the cafe.

"I'm a regular," he said. "Don't worry." He followed her to her trailer. "I'll set these in here," he said.

In the tiny space of her home, he seemed a large man. She had always thought of him as comfortably small, but she could not think where she had ever seen him outside of his house. She was herself a round, short woman. When they stood close together, she had to look up to him. She could not help thinking how different that must be for him, how unlike Rachel, who filled so much space.

He set one sack down on the table. She was still clutching the other one. He was looking over her shoulder at something. She craned her neck and saw that it was a photograph of her, Gustavo, and Gus as a baby.

"Your husband?"

Dulce nodded and set her sack down beside the other one. She turned to face the picture.

"He went to prison when Gus was four. He knifed a man in a fight, in a bar." She could hear Sandy breathing behind her. The Gustavo in the photograph was a figure from the distant past. How long was it before she stopped worrying, every hour, what was happening to him in that place? He told her she would forget. He said she would find another man. His parents wanted her to come to Texas with Gus, but she thought, then I'll never forget. She was so hurt, and she wanted her mother.

You said to forget, she thought, looking at the picture.

And now, was his stomach flat and hard? Was there bitterness in his eyes? Was he sorry he said, *forget?*

She turned around. Sandy was so close she felt the warmth of his breath on her forehead. "I'm losing Rachel and I don't know why," he said. He reached for her hand.

"I'm sorry," she said, though she had no feelings for them. She could not imagine why they should be unhappy.

He bent and kissed her lightly.

The surprise was not that he kissed her. The surprise was that the kiss suffused her with warmth and longing. She had no lover. She had no friends. Sometimes, when the need was great, she lay on her bed with her own hand against her body, but she did not think she longed for a man. She had told herself many times that Gustavo was a great love, although she understood that this was probably not so. He had been romance and escape. Alas he had also been selfish and cocky, and, in the end, stupid and unlucky.

"Oh!" Sandy gasped.

She shook her head.

He grasped her hand so hard it hurt. He pumped it up and down as he spoke. "I didn't mean—I didn't know I was going to—oh God, Dulce, I'm sorry."

She put her free hand over his busy one to still it. She lifted her head to kiss him again. She saw ahead only so far as that one kiss, but it was there, in front of her, and she needed it as the grass needs sun. He sighed and put his arms around her and pulled her close. He smelled of something bought, a cologne, a deodorant. He smelled of clean starched shirt. His mouth tasted of coffee. For a moment there was a promise between them of comfort. Solicitude. Simple gratification.

It was still early afternoon. School would not be out for an hour. His car was behind the cafe. No one would know.

She pulled away. "Please. Go home now."

Flustered, he waved his hands in front of him, making the sacks on the table rattle. For one ridiculous moment she thought he was going to try to put the groceries away.

"Dulce, you're like family," he said, though it had been half a year since he had spoken to her, even when she was there in his house, scrubbing his kitchen clean. "We've known each other a long time—"

"No," she said. "Not at all." She supposed she would never be able to set foot in their house again. Not a great loss.

He took out his wallet. "I want to give you something. I know it's rough. And now your car— Oh damn it to hell, I spent my cash at the store—"

He stood with his wallet open as if she might want to examine the contents. She took a step back, knocking against a chair.

"I didn't mean—don't think—" He shook his head miserably. She could still feel the print of his hands on her back.

Her face burned. She raised her hands to her cheeks. She felt suddenly lost between her two languages. She could find nothing to say to express her indignation and sadness. He put his wallet away and brushed the front of his shirt, as if for crumbs. The heat of her angry embarrassment had already burned off her surprise. She watched with disdain and pity as he fumbled to collect himself. She thought a man—an Anglo man—was a person who knew how to behave, a person who knew how to be in charge.

"It's all right," she said. She did not say his name.

"I mean it about the summer trip," he said. "Gus."

"Go home," she said. He stepped out, still looking at her. She shut the door.

She put some of the groceries in the refrigerator and left the rest in the sacks. She sat at the table and reinforced the buttons on her motel uniform. She had almost finished when she pricked her finger. Drops of blood bubbled up. She sucked her finger and stamped her foot. With one sweep of her arm, she sent the groceries flying. They were all over the floor when Gus came home.

He helped her pick it all up. There wasn't any way to explain to him what had happened. He was ten years old. She sensed his disdain, something new from him. She didn't know how to ask him, how have I disappointed you? She thought he looked frightened, too. There was less order in the world than he had thought. Maybe that was what growing up was, learning that nothing is firmly in place.

She baked the chicken and they ate in silence. While she did dishes, he showered and put on clean jeans.

She bit her lip to keep from telling him to put on pajamas. Lately, he had taken to dressing at night in the next day's clothes. It made his morning short work. Usually, she found it endearing.

"Sit down," she said. He was making her nervous, pacing in such a small space. He pulled the curtain aside to look out where there was nothing to see except other trailers. It was a hot evening, and he wore no shirt. His shoulders and arms were still round and soft with baby fat, but in his back he looked small, and his hips were slim. In another couple of years, he would begin to grow in earnest; he would fill out. He would have less and less to say to her. This was what she expected of a boy, though she had never lived with a brother. She had watched the boys in the barrio. She had watched their mothers.

"Sit down," she said again. He plopped down on the couch. His pillow and covers were still messy from the night before. She had an urge to straighten it all up. Instead, she sat across the room, the table between them. She said, "There are things about your father you should know."

His head jerked up, like an animal at a sound in the brush. "What things?" he said. His eyes had narrowed. There was a challenge in his gaze. *Watch what you say.*

"We were very young, Gustavo and me. When we married."

His chin jutted forward. He slumped against the back of the couch, his legs out, his knees bent toward one another clumsily. He said, "You never got a divorce."

She stared at the table. There were stains and burn marks in the veneer. She couldn't remember it ever being any better. The marks had been there when she moved in. It would be nice to have a new table, a table made of good wood.

She wanted to sit by him, but his gaze had a sheen of hostility in it. He thought she was going to say bad things about Gustavo. She only wanted him to have some realistic idea, any idea at all, what he was like. What he had been like.

"He'd left Texas and gone to a cousin's in L.A. He didn't have a steady job. We lived with other people. We never had any money."

"So?" He feigned boredom. Maybe he was bored. Maybe the details of grown-up life were too tedious to consider, at his age.

"He liked to drink with his buddies. He liked to drive around. He got in fights."

"I know what you're going to say. About him going to jail."

"That's where all that took him."

"You told me it wasn't his fault."

"I said he didn't mean to. I said it was the other man's knife. But it was his fault, too. He was drinking too much. He was arguing. He couldn't back off and let things be."

"I don't care! Everything is different now!"

"Time has passed," she conceded.

"He's not in jail anymore. I don't care about that."

"He left us all the time. He liked to be with his buddies. Other men." *He wanted a woman, not a wife.*

"I was a baby. Maybe he didn't like babies."

"I had to bring you home. I had to take care of you."

"There wasn't anything he could do, was there? From where he was? What was he supposed to do?!"

She couldn't remember why she had begun this. What she wanted Gus to know. She opened her hands, palms down, on the table, and stared at her knuckles. "I did what I could. I've always taken care of you."

"It's different now," he said again. "But you want me to be mad at him, because you are. Only, I'm not! I don't even remember him. What would I be mad at?"

"He's far away. His parole, it's to Texas, to his folks'."

"We could go there."

"It's not such an easy thing to pack up and move."

Gus looked around. He didn't have to say: *how much is there?* He said, "Why not? Hilario's family has lived that way his whole life. And he's happy."

There was no use in arguing this. Probably, Hilario was happy. Probably Hilario didn't know yet how tentative his life was here. But it hurt to hear Gus say Hilario was happy; what he meant was, he was not.

"I thought we were compadres," she said.

Gus jumped up. "Why do we live like this? Like we're the ones in prison? You work and come home. Who do you ever see? I don't even have grandparents. I don't have nobody but you."

"My mother—" Her jaw clenched. "My papa went to Mexico when I was little. I've told you." She was afraid she might cry.

"I wish I lived with Lupe! You think she's dumb, I know you do, but she's not. She talks to us. And I understand her. She doesn't care if she has to say things to me five times. She tells me about where they've lived. About Mexico. She tells me some day I'll have a family, too. And she tells me in Spanish!"

"Of course." It wasn't something she had ever thought about.

"I wish I lived with my dad."

"You don't know him. How can you say that?"

"I know he's my dad! Just because you don't love him, doesn't mean I don't." That chin up again. "Lupe says sangre es todo. Blood is everything. He's my father!"

Dulce reached over and picked up Gus' map of Texas. "He's a long long way away."

Gus grabbed the picture and crumpled it into a ball and threw it to the floor. He ran around, pulling pictures off the wall. "Gus," she pleaded. He threw his drawings around the room. He was sobbing.

Dulce got up and grabbed him. She tried to pull him to her, but he wouldn't let her. He turned and hunched in on himself. Helplessly, she said, "Sandy might take you to Portland next month. There's your scholarship. It'll be a nice summer."

Gus looked at her over his shoulder. "I want to go to Texas, Mama. I've got cousins there, don't I? A grandpa and grandma. Abuelos, Hilario says. He says they're the best."

"Not yet!" she cried. This was supposed to happen a long time from now.

"There's nothing here, Mama. Do you remember when you got me my new bike last year? And I rode it down through the new houses off of Main, where the streets are nice? And a policeman stopped me."

"Oh my sweet boy."

"He thought I stole it. He thought I was a poor Mexican kid and I took some Anglo kid's bike! I don't belong here. I hate it. I hate Lupine."

"Anglo kids get in trouble too."

"Not because they look Mexican, they don't."

She sat down heavily. "We'll write Gustavo about this summer. About you visiting."

"Sí, Mama," he said, and grinned. "Yo soy tu hijo. Y su hijo también."

She wouldn't cry. He was proud of himself. *Mi hijo.* He was a child. "But you're just a boy, Gus. I'm still your mother. You still belong with me. You come home to me."

Nora had made arrangements for lunch in a private room at the Anjou Restaurant. It was her treat. They dressed up for a celebration. Nora had run Carolyn Dannon's primary campaign for the Democratic nomination for the district's Congressional seat, against the man who had made a poor showing last time around. Now everybody was saying Dannon was dynamite. She was part of the new wave that might change the shape of Congress. Nora was feeling smug. Her life was full of brand new possibilities. Then too, she had sold a piece of property that had been in contention for nearly four years. A developer from California had wanted to build a golf course, but approval had been endlessly hung up; a second golf course didn't suit the sensibilities of the town just now, Nora said. Then there had been plans for houses, expensive ones, but the developer was called back for new hearings so many times he threw his hands up, forfeited funds, and fled to Idaho. Then Nora had made the ultimate sale, the result of her ingenuity and negotiation skills. A consortium had bought the property to build a language-immersion grade school. There had been talk about a replica of a medieval French village, too—say, Eze—as a fund-raising tourist attraction, but that had gone the way of the golf course. A school, though, that was perfect. "You wait," Nora said to them, not for the first time, "when Measure 5 kicks in, and property taxes for schools are curtailed; parents in this town will be racing for private alternatives. Some of them figured it out ahead of time. The Planning Commission sees it coming. *Ergo,* my biggest land sale." She poured champagne for everyone.

She looked spectacular, wearing a yellow linen dress with deep armholes. Maggie couldn't stop staring at her shoulders and arms. They were so *defined.* Lynn had tried to get them all to her gym, but she had convinced only Nora who, as Nora would, had achieved excellence and a new look. She had cut her hair so short it was shocking, but it looked great. Everybody made a fuss over it. Nora smiled chummily at Lynn and said, "I went down to L.A. with Lynn for a few days. Julia Roberts' hairdresser cut it." She smirked and said, "Go on, go on, have a good laugh, but it's true. And it was fun."

Maggie wondered how long lunch would run. She had told Polly an hour and a half. She felt dreadfully guilty, going off like this, but the plans had been made for nearly two weeks, and Polly said she should go, Gretchen was going, it would do her good. The baby Kendra had slept a little better Friday night, and Polly looked more rested. She had pulled the plastic tub out from the garage and set it on the patio with a couple of inches of water for Stevie to splash in, then moved the baby's crib out there, too. "We may just spend the day out here," Polly said, waving them away. Maggie thought she was being brave and generous, the way she always was. There was no guarantee both babies wouldn't start screaming five minutes after Maggie left. But Jay-Jay had been invited to play with Gus (a happy surprise), and Stevie was just one child, Polly's own grandchild, after all, and Maggie would have been crushed to be left out of the lunch. Gretchen had actually threatened not to go, herself, but Maggie made such a fuss about it, Gretchen said, okay, okay, and put on a new long T-shirt dress so tight her nipples poked out like thumbs.

Nora waved her hand. "We're all looking good." Maggie looked around, suddenly self-conscious and eager as a schoolgirl. She'd spent the last year letting her short thin hair grow to her shoulders, but it was so limp and uninspiring, she just pulled it back, or, on a special occasion like this, pinned it up in a flat twist. And, in a country where women starved themselves to be thin, she was, without trying, too skinny to look good. She smiled and wished she had worn something nicer than her bleached denim skirt, a skirt Polly had lent her to teach in and never got returned.

Rachel was wearing her Indian dress with bits of mirror all over the bodice. Lynn, beside her, was an opposite of style, in a simple, expensive, fawn-colored raw silk dress. Something about her was odd, but Maggie couldn't put a finger on it. She almost wished she had taken Lynn up on her offer, and gone to raid her cast-offs for something new (to her) to wear. She felt immensely out of place, aware that she was the odd one in this group, the least-educated, untraveled, most ordinary member. She tried to think what a character in a book would do.

She held up her glass. "To the group," she said. They toasted. Nora said, "To the year of the woman." She was always reminding them that they were a *critical mass.* Rachel said, "To the Muse," and Gretchen, sighing, said, "To fate." Lynn clicked her glass the loudest and said, "To food, ladies, that is what this is all about."

As if on cue the food began to arrive, served by their "waitperson Andrew." Andrew announced each dish, biting his consonants as if they were part of the fare. First they had eggplant caviar and baked mozzarella, followed by a sweet potato soup that surprised them with a touch of jalapeno. Nora had asked that everything be served family style.

They tasted and exclaimed and settled into eating. Lynn said she had been thinking of writing a cookbook. She didn't have enough to do. People were always raving about her food. When the group met at her house, they came earlier than usual because they knew there would be some fantastic array of dishes to try. "It would be around the theme of classic movies," she explained. "Couscous and roast lamb, *Casablanca.* Espresso and lobster, *Annie Hall.* You get the idea."

They all laughed. Maggie thought it was a ridiculous idea. Who would want to make a meal of espresso and lobster? She laughed with the others, of course. She stole a glance at Gretchen, whose laugh also sounded a little forced. Gretchen gave her a sly smile. They had sworn that, no matter what, they would not eat rabbit, for which the Anjou was famous. Not after seeing those poor rabbits skinned in *Roger and Me,* a movie she did not suppose Lynn would include in her cookbook.

While they waited for the main dish, Nora passed out a new brochure she had made up for Carolyn's campaign. Besides its exhortations to vote for Dannon, it had a snappy list of practical and urgent ways to "keep on doing the job women have to do." Things like checking "Ms." and joining the National Women's Mailing List. Challenging sexist slurs. There were twenty admonitions. On the front of the flyer, though, there were only these: GIVE TIME. GIVE MONEY. VOTE.

They looked over the pamphlet. Nobody wanted to challenge Nora—the booklet was fine—but nobody wanted to stand up and cheer, either. Nora's head-held-high expression made it clear that there was more coming, once that sank in. Maggie knew she would be leaning on them all summer about the campaign. Ever since the Clarence Thomas hearings, she'd been buzzing like someone born again. They had all been aghast and mesmerized and one hundred percent sympathetic with Anita Hill, but Nora was far gone. She had become political.

Nora talked for several minutes about the job of electing Dannon in a traditionally conservative district. She reminded them that in the last election, the district Democrat lost the state representative's seat by two hundred votes. They all listened politely, but nobody said anything. Maggie wondered if they all had the same thought, that they weren't there to celebrate; they were being enlisted.

"People think politics are about big-city slickos buying TV time and working tricky psychological moves," Nora said. The cords in her neck stood out. "But Carolyn Dannon is going to be elected because we are going to lick stamps and call voters and hand out pamphlets and make a difference." She let that sink in. "Women will elect her. You will elect her."

"Maybe we should get some more wine," Lynn said.

Maggie said, her voice hardly above a squeak, "I've got two kids."

Nora raised her eyebrows. "Which means you have three times as much at stake as a single person. Four, if you count Mo. Do you still count Mo?" She scratched her chin, pondering something. "Maggie, have you ever considered what it means that every member of your family has a name reduced to its diminutive?"

Maggie recoiled. Her eyes stung. She laid her napkin down and scooted her chair back.

Gretchen clasped her arm. "If you go, I'm going," she said.

"Wait, wait. This is not personal," Rachel said. "Is it?"

Maggie slumped back into her chair.

"*Sorry*," Nora said. Clearly, she was not. She looked around at them with her most penetrating gaze. "You are all for Carolyn, aren't you?"

Rachel said, "You know Sandy's family is staunch Republican. But you can count on my vote. Just don't expect a lot else. I'm going to finish my novel this summer." She seemed very pleased. "I've been awarded a residency on an island in the San Juans. Two months."

"Congratulations," Maggie said. She wondered what Sandy thought of that. She was relieved to leave the subject of her own marital status behind so quickly. Nora had already told her she thought she ought to divorce Mo. Maggie remembered exactly what she had said: A separation is not an egg to sit on.

Food arrived. Not rabbit. With some uneasiness, but an effort to smooth things over, they commented loudly and long on how good it all looked, much as they had commented on themselves.

Gretchen, whose eyes were red-rimmed, said wryly,

"Maybe we should talk about books." They smiled at one another, and dug into their *penne al tonno.* Gretchen pursued the matter. "After all, we are a book group."

"So who's reading what?" Lynn said. When nobody spoke up, she patted her mouth with her napkin and said, "I'll confess, I haven't read anything but magazines in a month." They had agreed to meet in May and set a new schedule for the rest of the year, one book each, then skip Christmas. "Dermott and I have been watching old movies. *My Life as a Dog.* He always watches that before he starts a new script. And *Chinatown.* Jack was never better than that."

"I've been running a political campaign," Nora said archly, as if she'd been accused of something.

Maggie chewed on her lip. "I've been trying to reread *Madness of a Seduced Woman.* It's one of my favorite books. But I get so sleepy, I'm only on page eighty-five." She didn't dare say how hard it had been lately. How reading hadn't quite fit in.

Gretchen said bitterly, "I haven't been reading, either, but there's time enough to read now."

Nora's eyebrows lifted. "School's out, I take it?"

"Phoebe has arrived, if that's what you mean," Gretchen said.

"Phoebe?" Lynn said. "Alex? Phoebe Alex?"

"You should reread *Madame Bovary,* Gretchen," Nora said. "Of course, she was the married one in that."

"I thought we were *au courant,*" Lynn said. Andrew brought the salad.

"We should look at some of the foreign writers," Nora said. "In a shrinking global world, we've got to face our diversities. Assimilation is an old and dead idea."

"You mean all those transistor radios in third-world countries will run out of batteries?" Gretchen said.

Maggie felt a headache starting at the base of her skull. She moved lettuce around on her plate. She had hoped, when she joined the book group, that their shared passion would make them friends. She had thought they *were* friends. "What I like," she said quietly, "is a book that enthralls you, makes a whole world you can't escape for days and days." She looked up boldly. "I really need that sometimes."

"What you like," Nora said, "is a book that comes together at the end." Once again, you could see she was criticizing.

Gretchen spoke up. "*Seduced Woman* is hardly a romance."

"I'm just saying maybe we ought to expand our views," Nora said. "I'd like to see us read writers from Ireland and Eastern Europe, India and Africa. I'd like to meet some challenge in our group."

"Like trekking in Turkey, you mean?" Gretchen said. She liked to read about women's adventures in exotic lands.

"I'd like to read something that made me laugh," Lynn said. She leaned back, smiling broadly, enjoying the sticks and stones. "I wouldn't mind having a good time with a book."

"As I said, I *have* been reading," Rachel said. "And I've brought a book to propose. It's my turn next." She reached into her large bag and brought out an anthology of lesbian writers on sexuality. She handed it to Maggie, who passed it to Gretchen, and on around the table.

"You really think we want to?" Lynn said.

Rachel said, "It's a wonderful collection. Provocative

and insightful, and, of course, sensual. If we're going to broaden our horizons, why do we have to go to Africa to do it? Why don't we consider experience other than our own, right here?"

Nora pushed her plate away. "I have to tell you I don't see myself having time for erotica, intellectual or not."

Rachel slid the book back into her bag. "Because it's by lesbians?"

"Are you telling us something?" Lynn asked.

Maggie was wondering the same thing. She'd never have asked, though.

Rachel said, "My sexual preferences are irrelevant. I'm proposing this book because it's good, because we haven't read anything by a gay writer—at least not anything about the experience of homosexuality—and because I think this group is getting as boring as the old one."

"My my," Nora said.

"That is your problem, though, isn't it?" Rachel said. "You are offended?"

"No, not at all," Nora said. "I don't want to read it because it's about sex. Any kind of sex. The idea that sex is its own subject, worth book after book—I have to tell you, it just doesn't interest me anymore."

"What ever happened to the personal as political?" Rachel asked.

Nora answered briskly. "That faded in about 1979." She gestured with her fork: eat, eat. They had all shoved their plates away by then. She made a show of spearing a slice of yellow pepper from the salad bowl, and held it in front of her like a baton. "Cities are becoming shells, Eastern Europe is roiling, Africans are starving—I'm sorry, Rachel, but things that drip and suck and swell and come just do not interest me."

Gretchen made a small gagging sound and coughed into her napkin. Lynn toyed with her glass. Rachel said, lightly, "You are a bitch, Nora." Maggie sank down in her chair. She didn't know whether this was a serious disagreement, or something between Nora and Rachel as insignificant as sibling grumbling. She didn't know if this was something friends did for fun. She remembered in high school she had heard girls going on at each other about boys and clothes and hair, sometimes viciously, then seen them hugging and laughing at the joke of it. She had been Gretchen's best friend in high school. They hadn't talked to one another like that. She wished Gretchen would get up now, take the lead to leave. She stared at Lynn across the table from her. Suddenly she realized what had been bothering her since their arrival. Lynn, who had been away several weeks in May, had done something with her eyes. What did they call it? A tuck? She didn't know whether to say anything, since Lynn had not mentioned it. What had she said? That she was going to a spa. A spa my eye, Maggie thought. She couldn't wait to ask Gretchen if she'd noticed.

Nora gave them all a cool appraising look, then sighed and spoke in a different voice altogether. "I apologize. I am in the worst mood I've been in since Craig left me for a woman who could sing. He's back, you know. I mean, really back. He and Trudy—imagine being named Trudy!—and the twins—imagine being a twin—now live four blocks away from Sarah and me. Five years he's a spectre; now he wants me to consider joint custody."

"Well, well," Rachel said. "Life is full of tales to tell."

"He called me in March about moving here. He wanted to know if I would find them a house. He said I might as well get the commission."

Lynn was delighted. "And did you?"

"I referred him to another agent in the office. He walked right into a house on Cathedral, about six lots up from you, Rachel. Get this. His mother-in-law died. In Santa Barbara. They sold her house, paid cash for this one, and have money left over. The sonofabitch."

"What does your lawyer say?" Lynn, who used to be a story consultant for a Hollywood studio, leaned her elbows on the table. "What's the chance of manslaughter versus Murder One?"

"Very funny," Nora said. "I talked to my lawyer, though. She said *he has the right.*"

"To joint custody!" Rachel exclaimed.

"No. To 'generous visitation arrangements.' Where was he when I needed some relief? Sarah turned eleven last week. We don't need him."

"What does Sarah say?" Gretchen asked. She sounded like someone speaking from under the bedclothes, her voice dull and heavy and muted. Maggie thought they ought to go. She wanted to go.

Nora was furious. "I think they had twins just to seduce her. To get out of child support. To make me mad." She smiled, a little, to show she was exaggerating.

Lynn said hotly, "Surely your lawyer can protect your support payments. Surely she can do that."

Nora drained the last of her wine. "Maybe we'll go with Carolyn Dannon to Washington next year. See how he likes that." She raised her empty glass in a mock toast. "And I do mean D.C."

"Whatever made you think we wanted to be friends with them?" Gretchen snarled as they walked toward the car. The others had stayed to try the desserts: poached pears, pot-a-creme, a raspberry tart.

"Something tells me the group just broke up," Maggie countered. She was a lot less sorry than she would have thought she would be. She was more worried about getting back to relieve Polly. Living in the puddle of someone else's graces—even Polly's—felt dicier all the time.

Gretchen said, "Drive up on Deer Creek Lane, I'll show you their house." Maggie didn't have the heart to say she ought to hurry. As she chugged up the long steep hill to that street, Gretchen said, "Shit, Maggie, doesn't love suck?"

Phoebe Alex's new house was at the dead end of Deer Creek Lane, just up the street from Lynn and Dermott's. And it was Phoebe's house, Gretchen made clear. Blake had explained it all. They weren't buying a quarter-million dollar house on his salary as a stage manager.

Maggie made a U-turn and parked across the street.

There wasn't a car in the drive, and the garage door was up.

"Blake's working matinee," Gretchen said.

They watched a woman in a turquoise velvet-terry track suit lope up the street. She did her end-of-the-run sprint right around Maggie's car, and they could see that she was at least seventy. She saw them watching and waved, smiling, then walked to the intersection and turned onto Spire, a street that dead-ended in forest. From a house on the corner another woman came out to walk her dog. She was carrying her cat up on her shoulder like a fur ruff.

Maggie had to ask. "Did you and Blake have some sort of—you know—goodbye scene?"

"Hardly. More like, lights down, up on a new act. New play."

"So where do you stand?"

"Let's go home. I have to work the break between matinee and the evening show."

"I'm sorry, Gretchen."

"He said I had to understand. Their history. They scraped by together. Now Phoebe's getting rich and famous, he can't walk out on her."

"He thinks he's entitled to some of it?"

Gretchen shot Maggie a hateful look. "He thinks she'll fall apart. She'll say, 'What was it all for?' And look, the house is in Lupine. It's perfect. A two-hour flight to L.A. She can have her career, and she can have Blake and Lupine. Maybe she can have a baby." She made a terrible, retching, crying sound. "Can't you see it now? There'll be a dance for the company, but they'll invite her too, because she's famous. She'll walk among us, acting humble, like all actors are equal, huh? At the end of the season, when we light candles and hold hands and sing 'Greensleeves,' she'll want to be there. She'll say it just kills her to be in the movies and not in a company like ours. She'll act like she knows she's sold out but it just cannot be helped. She'll kiss everyone on both cheeks. She'll sing something cheerful at our AIDS benefit. She'll buy a festival sponsorship, and hold court in the Members' Lounge, where I will have to serve her coffee!"

"She won't," said Maggie. She tried to steal a look at her watch. She still had to pick up Jay at Dulce's.

"She'll be in the movies, then she'll come to Lupine just to fart around."

"She won't," Maggie said again.

"Blake farts," Gretchen said. "He has this terrible problem with flatulence. In bed. Every time." She laughed. "Hell, let's go home."

She pulled up in front of the house, to let Gretchen out. Gretchen had laughed, more or less, all the way down the hill from Deer Creek Lane, then had cried the rest of the way home. It made Maggie too nervous to drive and talk seriously, so she didn't try, but she reached over to keep Gretchen in the car a minute. She turned off the ignition. "I'm sorry about Blake," she said. "About you being hurt."

"Yeah, well." Gretchen's hand was on the door handle.

"You know I love you."

"Yeah, well."

"Gretchen, come on. Look at me. I'm your best friend. I know how you must feel."

Of course she meant to comfort. She couldn't have been more surprised when Gretchen whirled her head around and snarled at her. "Of course you don't! How could you? I am a stupid cunt in love with a man who is married to somebody else!"

"I only meant—"

"Oh, you're so stupid! My brother loves you!"

"Why are you yelling at me?"

"You want *me* to feel what *you* feel. That's what you really mean. Well, I can't. All my feelings are busy right now!"

"Gretchen—" she tried to stop her, but Gretchen got out of the car and slammed the door. She watched her all the way to the house. She wanted to follow her and talk, but she had places to go and things to do. She had to be mother. She had to be.

The boys were missing. Maggie had told Jay she wanted him home by two. It was past three, and there was no sign of him. She went to Dulce's. They left a note on Dulce's door and went off in Maggie's car to look in likely places. First they checked at Lupe's. Gus and Jay had come by for Hilario a little before noon, and they had gone off on their bikes (Hilario on the ancient one the station owner had lent him). From Lupe's, Maggie and Dulce scouted spots along the creek, and the big ditch under the freeway near Maggie's house where, this time of the year, a thousand things were growing and sprouting and begging to be explored. They went by Rachel's house and Maggie ran in to see if Mason had seen them. Finally, Maggie said she had to get home. Jay was on his bike, it was only mid-afternoon, but she was angry with him for his tardiness. Dulce said Gus and Hilario often spent the day away, but conceded that Maggie had set a time. "I always want to know where he is," Maggie said, a little defensively. Dulce said, "I used to be like that."

When Maggie went home again and told Polly where she'd been—she went in talking, before Polly could say anything about her being late—Polly immediately said, "But don't you think he—" and at exactly that same moment, Maggie realized where they would have gone. Jay would have something to show off, something to share. How stupid not to have thought of it in the first place.

"He has this spot where he liked to go with his dad last year." She had asked Dulce to ride over with her. "It's a pretty piece of property, not very far, but they don't have any business being there." She confessed that she had gone there herself earlier in the week, trying to cheer Jay up. "He looks at me a way, sometimes, it makes me want to scream. We have to get out of the house." Dulce, maddeningly, said nothing.

At the intersection by the junior high, they had to wait for a line of a dozen or more bicyclists to pass. They were all dressed alike, in white helmets and T-shirts and lemon yellow tight shorts. They were in their fifties, maybe their sixties, trim as sticks, and Maggie was so fascinated, she let a car half a block away pass before she inched forward to turn. A driver behind her honked. "Okay!" she yelled, then glanced at Dulce, who had no expression at all.

As they turned onto the street where the Gabrelli property was, though, Dulce whispered, "*Mother of God.* Not up there," pointing toward the Gabrelli house.

A fire truck was parked in the yard, and a police car at the street. Maggie pulled in beside the car and jumped out. The three boys were in the back, huddled like sick little birds on the seat. Maggie tried the door handle. Of course it was locked. She turned to Dulce, but Dulce wasn't behind her; she was still standing by the car, her hands covering her mouth. Jay saw Maggie. His eyes widened, and he started crying. His poor broken-out face was puffed and red. Gus glanced up, then hung his head. Hilario yawned and leaned against the back seat, as if this was all so boring. It was an act. Maggie thought, I bet he's scared to death.

She banged on the window. "What have you done?"

"Ma'am," someone said behind her. It was a policeman. She recognized him. He often sat at the busy intersection kids had to cross in the morning near the grade school. He had a round, friendly face and freckles. He was younger than she was. He looked like a kid trying to play grown-up, his face so serious, his shoulders pulled back bravely.

Another cop was striding across the yard toward them. The engine of the fire truck turned over, and Maggie jumped at the noise. Slowly, the truck pulled out and away. Whatever had been going on seemed to be over.

Dulce had moved next to Maggie. At the same moment, they reached for one another, clasped hands, and squeezed hard.

As the second policeman approached, the first introduced himself—Officer Brandon—and suggested they step away from the car. Maggie glanced at her son, whose swollen face was glossy with tears, then followed the cop a few yards away, toward the farm house. What had been going on while she was eating eggplant caviar?

They're all right, she told herself. Nobody dies of crying. She ought to know!

"Are you the boys' mothers?" the officer asked. Maggie nodded. He looked at Dulce, who said, "Yes." The officer took out a pad and pen and took their names. Maggie was dressed up, from the lunch. Dulce was wearing an old pair of jeans and a T-shirt. Maggie wished they were dressed more alike. She hoped Dulce wasn't uncomfortable. Uncomfortable! Their kids locked in a cop car.

"You knew they were here? You know this is private property?" The officer directed his question to Dulce. Maggie tried to explain—Jay's dad had worked here in the summer, he had been told it was okay to play. The officer looked doubtful. He said, "We were about to take them to the station and give you a call. They're very lucky, you know, not to be hurt. You're very lucky. That's the thing, boys this age, playing unsupervised."

Maggie's cheeks felt scorched in the sun, under his scolding gaze. Did he really think mothers stood around and watched nine-year-old boys all day? "What happened?" she asked. She had a sensation of choking. She tried to swallow, but couldn't make her throat work. She panicked, for an instant, and then she squeezed Dulce's hand again and made herself stop trying to swallow. "What did they do?" She glanced beyond the cop, toward the far part of the property. She didn't see any signs of a fire.

Officer Brandon explained that the boys had built a fire in the shed to roast hot dogs. They made some effort to put it out, but left it smoldering. Then they went up the slope where the abandoned cars were parked, to fool around. He shook his head. "Boys," he said. "They love cars." He shook his head again. "These old cars ought to be hauled away. You see 'em all over. I bet they've been here thirty years. Course, they're not expecting anybody to be trying a joy-ride in them, are they?"

From where they stood, Maggie couldn't see the police car. She thought the officer had deliberately placed them like that. It was a kind of torture. "They're not hurt?" she said. It required enormous effort to keep from crying. She wished she had brought Polly. Of course she hadn't known there was going to be trouble. Of course Polly had her hands full with two babies.

"Oh," she said. She was nauseated. The ground seemed to be unstable beneath her feet. She wished Mrs. Cecil was there. A principal would know how to handle something like this. She'd know the boys hadn't meant any harm.

Dulce put her arm around her shoulders. "They're okay," she said.

"The Mexican boy—the little one—" the policeman said. "He was in the car."

"Gus," Dulce said.

"The other two pushed it off, a little roll off that slope, a little ride. The car hit the corner of the shed, glanced off that fallen roof, and slid to a stop." His look grew sterner. "Very lucky," he said. "It must have shook him pretty good, but it didn't do him any significant damage." He touched his chin. "Gave him a little nick here, the steering wheel. Maybe some bruises. We looked him over pretty good."

Maggie looked at Dulce. She thought Dulce had to be alarmed, but she kept her face utterly neutral, as if she had turned to stone.

"The impact of the car shook the shed roof, and some lumber shifted. The coals sparked. There was a fire."

"Oh God." Maggie tasted tuna and jalapeño and the sour tang of wine in her throat.

"It didn't amount to much. The neighbor across the road came out when he heard the car hit, and saw smoke. Called the fire department and us."

"The car?" Dulce said. "It's wrecked?"

"The car's junk, ma'am. The car didn't matter. Old Willys, can you believe it? If somebody had taken care of it, it'd be worth something. Rusted out, though. Nothing worth salvaging." Maggie remembered Mo saying the same thing. Too bad, he said. He had always wanted an old car.

"And nothing burned?" Dulce said.

"No ma'am, few scraps of wood." Once again, he said, "Lucky thing." Maggie coughed. Her throat was hurting. He said, "Good thing we had that little rain this week, the grass has been so dry. Might have been quite a little brush fire, if things had gone badly."

"But they didn't," Dulce said calmly. "Officer, can we take the boys?"

"One thing," he said. "The big kid. Whose kid is he? He won't say anything. He speak English?"

Dulce said, "He's my sister's son. He's probably scared. Hilario Hinojosa. Of course he speaks English. He's bilingual." Maggie couldn't help staring at her, but Dulce didn't pay any attention. Obviously, she had her reasons to lie.

"I think we better take him home," the policeman said.

"They're not home," Dulce said quickly. "His parents aren't there. He's staying with me over the weekend."

He looked at her for a moment, one eyebrow raised slightly. "How's that?"

"They've gone to Salem," Dulce said. "To see my mother."

He poised his pen over the pad. "What's their address, ma'am?"

"They're staying with me. They're just moving, so they're staying with me right now."

"I'm going to need to talk to his folks."

"Oh sure. Monday. They'll be back then."

He put the pad away. Maggie didn't think he was especially satisfied, but nothing Dulce had said was unreasonable. Family did stay with one another. Especially poor people, and he wouldn't have any trouble thinking of Dulce as poor. He didn't have any reason to be suspicious. He didn't know two families couldn't fit in Dulce's place.

They walked back to the car. The other policeman was leaning against it, chewing on a toothpick. Jay called out. "Mom!" Maggie's heart jumped. "Please," she said.

Officer Brandon opened the door and the boys crawled out slowly. Jay threw his arms around his mother. Gus rubbed his eyes and stood back. Hilario stood, his head cocked a little, his eyes hooded and sullen and older than a boy's eyes should be.

Brandon said, "I'm going to let you boys go with your mothers now. You'll be getting letters. I think someone will want to talk to you."

Jay clung to Maggie.

"And there'll be some damages."

"Oh God," Maggie said. "The car?"

"We're trying to get hold of the owners here. They're in Concord, California. I imagine they'll want to have the car towed away to the junk yard. I think you'll have to pay for that."

Dulce said, "Of course."

"The shed—" He shrugged. "It's negligible. I don't know why he's left it there."

"My bike," Gus said. They all turned toward him.

Officer Brandon made a sucking noise. "They're up

by the shed. Why don't you boys go get them and we'll put them in the trunk?"

Maggie and the policemen stared at one another uncomfortably. Dulce got in the front seat of the car, leaving the car door open.

Jay's and Gus's bikes fit in the trunk, but of course it wouldn't close. The second policeman rummaged and found a piece of rope in the car. Hilario stood to one side with his hands on his bike's handlebars. He still hadn't spoken since the women arrived.

"It's not far," Maggie said. "He can ride his bicycle."

"Yeah, okay," Officer Brandon said. The second policeman announced that the trunk was secure. He gave the lid a sound pat. Brandon looked like something was still bothering him.

"I go?" Hilario finally said. He had been following everything.

"You've got no business in a car," Brandon told him. "Next time I suppose you'll steal one that runs."

Hilario said, "Cabrón." Gus gasped.

The policeman said, "I don't speak Spanish, but I'm not stupid, kid. How old are you?"

Hilario said, "Thirteen."

"I could take you in to juvey, you know. This could be a bigger thing."

Maggie didn't think Hilario understood. He stood still, but he didn't look cowed now, with his bike between his legs, his feet planted square in the dirt. "Thank you, mister," he said.

"Phht!" the policeman said. He turned and walked briskly back to his car and got in on the driver's side. Maggie and the boys hadn't moved. He leaned his head out of the police car. "Watch whose yard you fool around in," he said. "Somebody just might shoot you." He spun the wheels, digging out in reverse.

The boys rode in the back seat. Dulce hadn't said anything to Gus, so Maggie thought, I can wait, too. I won't get all excited right now. She couldn't imagine what Polly would say. A fireman's grandson, starting a vandal's fire!

At the trailer, Dulce said, "It sounds like it was Gus' fault. I'll pay for the towing."

"It wasn't all my fault!" Gus said. Dulce gave him a hard look.

"I'm sure it was Jay's idea," Maggie said. "Anyway, they did it all together."

"Lupe doesn't have any money," Dulce said.

"No," Maggie said.

Dulce shrugged. "Let's see what they say. What're they going to do? Put us in jail?"

It didn't feel right between them, Maggie thought. There was something she needed to say, but she didn't know what it was. "I'll talk to you," she said. Dulce nodded, and walked into the trailer behind her son.

"How could you?!" Maggie shrieked, once the car was parked in Polly's driveway. All the tension of the looking, the scare of seeing those official cars in the Gabrelli yard, the vision of her son in the back of a police cruiser—it all erupted. She grabbed his shoulder and shook him. He slapped her arm and ran into the house. Coming in behind him, she heard Stevie and the baby both screeching.

Polly was walking back and forth, holding the baby up in front of her, gently rocking her up and down, while talking softly. Stevie ran up to Maggie and hit her on the leg with a wooden spoon. Maggie yelped, jumped back, then bent over to pick her up. She was hot and sweaty. She needed changing. Anger flushed through Maggie. How could Polly let her get like this?

Six feet away, Polly was now singing, "Mama's gonna buy you a diamond ring" softly to Kendra.

"We'll go," Maggie said sharply.

Kendra had stopped screaming. Polly pulled her to her chest and spoke. "Don't. I want to know what happened."

Jay had already gone down the hall and slammed the bedroom door. They could hear him sobbing. Maggie blurted out the details: the fire, the car, the humiliation of the police.

Polly said, "You could run out for a pizza after a while. We could rent a movie. Let me get Kendra down."

Maggie took Stevie down to Polly's room to change her. Gretchen was at work. Stevie was fussing, but had lost steam. Maggie, with a willed effort, played a bit of peekaboo and tickle-belly to cheer her up. She took her in the bathroom and washed her face, gave her a hug and a pat on the bottom, and sent her toddling back toward the living room. "Baby!" Stevie said.

Maggie sank down onto the bathroom floor. Tears ran down her face. She was humiliated by the policeman's dressing-down: you aren't doing your job, you aren't a good mother. She was doing the best she could!

Maybe, when Mo called, she would tell him: Come get him.

Maybe.

How could Jay push her to this? What was wrong with him?

She heard Polly padding back and forth in the hall. The baby, now in her crib, made staccato squeaking sounds, then fell quiet. Maggie knew she ought to get up and do something, but she couldn't make her limbs work. And she didn't know what to say to her son. He had betrayed her, doing the very thing she had warned him not to do, with that stupid fire. And a car!

She reached for a towel and held it balled up against her face.

She heard Polly go into the room where Jay was, directly across the hall. She left the door open.

Jay let out a cry which was then muffled. Maggie knew he had thrown his face into his grandmother's lap, which was just what she would have liked to do.

"Now, you're not hurt," she heard Polly say. She couldn't hear Jay's low voice in reply.

"I know it was an accident," Polly said. "A *didn't-mean-to* accident. But not an *out-of-the-blue* accident. Not an *entirely-unasked-for* accident."

Jay's protest was short and whining.

"Listen, Jay-Jay, you're okay, you didn't get hurt, that's the main thing. But you have to think about what you're doing. Not what happened today, I don't mean that. You three boys cooked up an adventure and it got out of hand. I mean all this crying and pouting and acting mean to your mother. You have to act nicer. Your mother needs for you to be more grown-up. You need to treat her better. You need to help me take care of her."

Maggie pressed the towel against her mouth to keep from crying out. She got up, shut the door, and sat down on the side of the tub. *You have to help me take care of your mother.* She could have died of shame. Jay is *nine years old*, she thought. He needs more than a loss group. He needs a mother who's stopped being a baby. He needs parents who are all grown-up.

She washed her face and brushed her hair, then stepped across the hall to look in on him. He was asleep, or was pretending to be. He looked especially young, curled up. She put her palm on his forehead. His eyelids jumped.

She sat down beside him. "Jay-Jay, listen to me. I'm your mother. You don't have to take care of me. You don't have to worry about me at all. *I'll* take care of *you*, do you hear? Me and your daddy. We'll take care of you. Don't worry. Don't think about anything. I'm going to make it better. Mo and I are going to take care of you. Not because you did something bad, or because you're angry. Because we love you, and we love Stevie, and we love each other."

He still didn't move or open his eyes. Maybe he was asleep after all. If so, he must have been dreaming, to twitch so.

She went into the kitchen. Stevie had crawled up on the couch with a teddy bear and fallen asleep, her rump in the air. Polly was at the table, drinking a glass of apple juice. She looked terribly tired. "Sit down, honey," she said. "Want some juice?"

"He didn't do anything awful," Maggie said.

"Of course he didn't. He's a little boy. They like to scare them, though. I think they think of it as inoculation."

"It wasn't like he hurt someone or stole something."

"I could tell you stories about Mo," Polly said.

"We need to talk about Mo," Maggie said.

Polly nodded.

"I miss him."

"I know. I miss him too. But a mother, well, a mother is supposed to. It's okay. You, though, the children—"

"I know. I'm ashamed of what I've put you through."

"Nothing. You've done nothing. You've done what you could."

"I've been such a baby." She couldn't help it, the damned tears started again. "You are—like—" It was hard to say. "Polly, you know you are my mother."

"I'm not her, Maggie. But I love you. And I'll love you when you go back to my son. I'll love you when you make your own family."

"Do you think I can?"

Polly took a moment to answer. "There were times

when I didn't think I loved Morris anymore. In the middle years. I didn't understand that there are—these spaces—in a marriage. It scared me, until I'd gone through them and learned I could. But these times, when I didn't know about him? About my husband? I still loved the unit. The family. I always loved the family."

"I wouldn't want to move all the way to Texas because it's too hard to be a single mother. Lots of women do it. I could, too."

"You could. And would you *not* go to him, just to prove you could? Would that be a reason?"

Jay came stumbling in, rubbing his eyes. "I'm hungry," he said.

Maggie smiled at him. "I thought you had hot dogs."

It took Jay a moment to assess this. He saw his mother's smile, though. "They burned," he said.

Maggie got up. "Why don't I take you over for a taco? And then we'll go to the store. I'll make dinner." She bent and kissed Polly on the cheek. "You ought to grab a nap while you can."

"Ahh, what an idea," Polly said. She headed for the couch. "Stevie won't mind." She scooted the baby over and stretched out.

* * *

In the town where I grew up there was a low bridge across the river. I didn't live there after I was twelve, but I went back once, when I was fourteen. I was with a group of kids from the church, my foster parents' church, and we had been swimming along the bank. The water was quiet there, that whole stretch. From where we were we could see the old school where I would have gone to junior high if I'd stayed.

It must have been five, five-thirty in the evening, which, in late summer, was still hot and bright. I was bored with the swimming, with the group. They had started singing "contemporary Christian songs," which they learned at church. The church had a charismatic minister who lifted weights and wore skin-tight jersey shirts to show the results. He brought in performers every month or so, pretty people who sang about Jesus and raised their arms and smiled and showed huge white teeth. They were very tedious. I used to get through the services, and the performances, by imagining myself doing something shocking, like taking off my clothes and running down the aisles, or hunkering down and peeing for Jesus.

I didn't feel anything for Jesus, and I didn't like to sing. I didn't like my foster family. I was angry at my mother.

I left the group and walked up onto the school grounds for a while, and then back onto the bridge above where they were gathered. I was facing the sun, and I couldn't really see them, they were washed out in the light. The water and the banks and the river stretching out past where it could be seen—all these things looked like something done in watercolor. It was pretty. I stopped thinking or feeling for a few moments; I just looked at the color and light.

There was a beautiful old sycamore high on the bank above where the kids were gathered. At the top it seemed to shimmer. Once I looked at it, I couldn't seem to look away. I stopped hearing the laughter and singing below; I didn't even hear the occasional car passing behind me on the bridge. It was like I had moved over, across that space, onto the tree itself, and I was seeing something I had never seen before, only it had no form, it was, simply, light.

Not long after, I read a book about angels. I couldn't stop thinking that the light I had seen that day, high on the tree above the river, had had a shape after all, had been something real and not-real and important and special. It was nothing, I know, a play of light, but it helped to think of it as something given to me, apart from the life I was living. I thought of it as a gift from my mother. I can't tell you why; it didn't make sense to me, even then, but it made me feel better. It made me stop being angry. It gave me a new way to feel.

"You want to talk Spanish? How about loco? Try estúpido!" Dulce spoke furiously as she dabbed at her son's face. He was going to have a black eye, and the skin had been broken open on his chin. She ran into the bathroom, threw open the medicine cabinet, and tossed bottles and boxes into the sink. She found Merthiolate and Band-Aids and went back to doctor him.

"Ow!" he protested.

"You'll think ow," she said. "You'll wish ow."

"Aw ma, what'd we do that was so bad?"

"What you did was you called attention to yourself, you stupid boy. I heard him. 'The little Mexican kid,' he called you. 'The big Mexican kid,' he called Hilario."

"So?"

"So that's how he thought of you. How he remembers you. You think if you were a few years older he'd have sent you home? Maybe not even if it'd been just me and not Maggie, not an Anglo with a car and another kid. If this'd been L.A., you bet you'd be in detention. Or shot."

"It's not L.A. Lupine is sure not L.A."

"No? Well, isn't Lupine where—you're the one brought this up last night—where a 'little Mexican kid' can get harassed for riding his own goddamned bicycle?"

"I'm sorry." She thought maybe he was. Sorry she was mad at him, anyway.

She put her hands on the sides of his face and kissed one cheek, then the other. She kissed his forehead.

"*Ma.*"

She sat down. "You learn something from this, Gus. You don't call attention to yourself."

"Okay."

"And that's not the only risk you took. Going downhill in a car you can't control? You don't know about a car. You didn't know what would happen."

"It was just a big open field, Mama, except for the shed."

"Was it Hilario's idea?"

"No. He said we didn't need to be in it. He just wanted to see it roll. He said we could just watch, see where it would stop. But Hilario's lived in five states and Mexico, Mama. He's had all kinds of adventures. I thought, here's mine. Like somebody on a track. And it was fun. Even the crash was fun."

"Ohhh," she groaned. "Adventure." She pushed his hair back off his forehead. "Change your shirt. We're going to go see Hilario. And Lupe. You have to see what your adventure means to them."

Lupe was sobbing. When she saw Dulce come in the door, she wailed. She cried to the Virgin, she cried for her own mother, she cried for Cipriano, who was so far away he didn't even know.

Hilario sat in the corner of their saggy little sofa, looking half buried in it, and sullen. Gus held a hand up in greeting. Hilario gave the slightest nod. There seemed to be children everywhere, the baby crawling, the middle two running around a little crazy. Everyone was upset.

"Shhh. Calm yourself," Dulce said. She took Lupe to the table and they sat down. She held her hands. The baby crawled over.

"What will they do to my boy?" Lupe wept. She picked up the child and held her to her chest.

"They won't do anything. He didn't commit a crime. It's not that. It's that they'll want to see you. They'll come around."

Lupe stopped crying. "They'll want to see papers." The baby settled down on her lap.

"Yes, when they see you don't speak English. When they see—well, when they see all of you."

"Oh, my babies," Lupe said.

"Can you get hold of Cipriano? Is there a way to call him?"

"Sí. I can call his brother, and he goes to him, he can take a message."

"You can't stay."

Lupe bit her lip.

"They'll deport you."

"Sí."

"With your babies."

"Oh Hilario!" Lupe cried.

"I told them he's my nephew. I said his parents would be gone all weekend. They'll come around on Monday. I work. It'll be afternoon. I'll tell them things."

Lupe's hands came up, she covered her face. "Oh, oh," she wept. The baby began crying, too.

"Is there somewhere you can go? Until Cipriano comes?"

Lupe's hands came down. "My sister, she is in Hemet, California, it's a long way."

"How soon could you be ready? Could you be ready tomorrow?"

Dulce looked around the little trailer. They couldn't carry everything, but they could get out. Lupe was bereft. "My little house," she said.

"They will come around. They will want papers. They will send you to Mexico." Dulce paused. "Maybe that would be good. They send you home?"

Lupe pointed to Hilario. "My boy is learning English well. He is good in the math in school."

"Then you must go."

Lupe shook her head. "But I have no money."

Dulce reached into her pocket. She held up some folded bills. "I'll ask Maggie to drive me to get you tickets, all of you. I think this will get you to Hemet. Does your sister have a phone?"

"For certain she has a phone. She is a teacher's aide in a school," Lupe said proudly.

"Then you must go and call her. At the station, there's a pay phone. I would take you to my house, but we are walking. My car—" she shrugged, then held her arms out for the baby.

That night, Maggie called. An exhausted Gus had already gone to bed. Dulce had heard him crying, then he fell asleep.

After she hung up, she went over and knelt down by him.

"Gus, dear Gus, wake up."

He moaned.

"Turn over, I have something to tell you."

He pulled himself up. "Is something else wrong?"

She thought: He's crying about Hilario.

"No, not wrong." She took his hands. "That was Maggie. Jay's father is going to come for him, the day after school is out. They have offered to take you back with them. To your father. They have offered you a ride to Texas."

Her heart went out to him. "Oh Mama!" he said, and then his face fell. "And you'll be in Oregon."

"Oh no," she said. She took him in her arms. She rubbed her face against his hair. "I will not send you to Texas alone. I'm not living here without my son."

* * *

Dulce says: I dream of a girl with hair as black as currants. She reads to me from her dream-book.

The girl is in a house. The house, once beautiful, is old and decaying. It is two stories, made of stones, with many rooms. The girl's mother moves through the rooms, closing the door and windows, except the kitchen, downstairs, and, upstairs, a bedroom with a tiny balcony.

The girl lies on a bed at dawn, her body covered by a finely woven white cotton blanket. Her long black hair spills across the pillow and sheet and onto the floor beside her.

Below her, in the orchard, a man is singing:

> *Despierta, mi bien, despierta.*
> *mira que ya amaneció;*
> *ya los parajitos cantan,*
> *la luna ya se metió.*
>
> *The moon has gone down.*

She rises and pulls over her head a white smock with an embroidered bodice. She twists her hair into a rope and loops it below her shoulders.

The singing goes on.

She moves onto the tiny balcony and watches the sun rising over the hills. Across from her the pear trees are in blossom. To look across the orchard is to scan a sea of white.

Qué bonita, mi querida.

She gazes down on a young man standing at the foot of the nearest tree. He wears white pajama bottoms and a red scarf twisted and tied on his forehead. He reaches up and extends his arm. She leans over to see him better. His chest is bare and brown.

Oh love! her heart sighs. A shaft of fresh sunlight strikes her face and she raises her hand to shield her eyes. For a moment the man is lost to her and she gasps. But she hears him again.

Qué bonita, mi querida.

Behind her she hears her mother's voice. Below she hears the man's. Come away! her mother calls. Come away! he calls.

She bends over, as far as she dares, her arm stretched toward him.

Her mother cries: Come away!

A light wind moves the dress against her body.

Come away! he cries.

The house groans and pulls up higher above the orchard. The terrible space between the girl's hand and the hand of the man with the red bandana grows wide.

Aiee! both of them cry.

She weeps and tosses her head, until the thick dark mass

of her hair falls out of its twist, and cascades over her shoulders and down her back.

Your hair! he cries. Your hair!

She leans over and her hair spills over the balcony and onto his head and shoulders. Her heart thrums. As he climbs, she sings:

Qué bonita mañanita,
como que quiera llover.

What a beautiful morning,
as if it might rain.

Now her mother shrieks, the house shudders, birds cry, but up, up comes her love to her on the rope of her hair.

Under her smock, her brown round body yearns for him.

Across from the balcony the tree stretches out its limbs and the girl and the young man climb onto one. Below the canopy of blossoms, the tree is heavy with fruits in many colors, and the air is sweet with their smell.

They sit on a limb, red and orange globes of fruit lying in the pouch her dress makes between her legs. The limb breaks away without a sound and carries them from the closed-off house, the mother's cries, toward sunlight.

The girl's breasts swell and press against the cloth of her dress; the flat plane of her belly rounds; a woman's breasts, a woman's belly; the caress of a breeze, the weight of the flesh of fruit, the blush of a woman's skin, the heat of a man's gaze.

June 1992

* * *

Maggie drove Dulce and Gus to Dulce's mother's house the morning before they left. She had brought a paperback book to read. "Take all the time you need," she said, holding it up. "These may be the last calm moments I have for a long time." She gave Dulce a thumbs-up, good-luck sign.

Gus was all dressed up in a starched white shirt and pressed jeans. His hair was combed wet and slicked back. He looked a little bewildered. Dulce had worn a cotton print dress, and had taken the extra time to French-braid her hair down her back. She wore lipstick. She wore a little cross on a chain around her neck.

The house was in a nice development above the hospital, in a town twelve miles away. The lawn was green and bordered with flower beds. A blue jeep sat in the driveway. It was early afternoon; her mother had said she would be going to the hospital at three. She had suggested one. Dulce thought it was her way of saying they wouldn't take long.

She rang the doorbell, expecting her mother to answer, but it was her sister, Karen, instead. She had not seen her since she was a little girl. Now, at eleven, she was tall and very pretty, with short curly hair. She was dressed in white jeans and a tank top. She had carefully arched, plucked eyebrows. She held the door open for an awkward moment, then stepped back and waved them in. Across the large room, Dulce's mother walked toward them. She was dressed in the white pants she wore to work, with a pale blue blouse. She was wearing her hair shorter than Dulce had ever seen it.

"Come in," her mother said. "And Gus!" she added brightly. She did not embrace Dulce, nor even reach for her hand. Instead, she gestured toward the furniture arrangement in front of an ornate fireplace. Dulce and Gus sat down on the couch. Dulce's mother sat on a chair. Dulce looked around. Karen had disappeared.

"My, what a big boy you've become," Dulce's mother said. Gus stared at his knees.

"You look well," Dulce said.

"We're all fine," her mother replied.

"Karen is a beautiful girl."

Her mother smiled. "And Gus, you're such a handsome boy. Do you do good in school?"

Gus looked at Dulce. Dulce said, "He's a good student, Mother. School isn't hard for him."

"Yes, well, what is this about the trailer? You said on the phone—you're going out of town?"

"We're leaving, Mother. We're going to Texas. I told you. Gustavo is in Texas now."

"I thought you were divorced." Dulce's mother glanced at Gus, then back at Dulce. "I thought that happened a long time ago."

"I never told you I was divorced."

"I assumed."

"I've brought you the keys, and the title, to the trailer." Dulce opened her bag and took them out. She laid them on the glass top of the coffee table in front of her. Her mother looked at them oddly, as if something dirty had climbed up there.

"Whatever for?" she asked Dulce.

"I want to return the trailer to you, that's all. You can sell it."

"How do you know? What if you need it again?"

"I'm leaving Oregon, Mother. I'm going to live in Texas."

"I wouldn't know—"

"Thank you for the trailer. I don't know what we'd have done, especially at first."

Dulce's mother observed her almost suspiciously. Perhaps she thought Dulce was being sarcastic? But it was true; she did not know what she would have done, since she could not live with her mother. Since she had had no skills, no money, and a small son.

"And there's something I want to ask you about."

"Yes?"

"About Papa. I want to talk about Papa."

"How odd," her mother said.

"It isn't odd at all. He's my father, and I have questions."

Her mother's eyes darted back and forth: Dulce, Gus, Dulce, Gus. She said, "Gus, would you like something to drink? In the kitchen, you could help yourself from the fridge."

Gus looked at his mother, who said, "Why don't you go and wait in the car with Maggie?" He nearly leapt to his feet. "Tell your grandmother goodbye," she said.

Her mother smiled broadly. "So nice to see you, Gus." No one could possibly believe it.

Gus mumbled something and fled.

Dulce and her mother stared at one another.

A funny expression flitted across her mother's face.

Dulce said, "He looks very Mexican."

Her mother said, "Yes."

"I knew you were thinking that."

"Actually, I was thinking he looks like Salvador. Maybe he looks like his father, I don't remember what he looked like."

"I thought maybe he looked like Papa."

"I don't know where he is, you know. I've never heard." She waved her hand. "Zacatecas. I was never there. He wanted us to go. Someday we'll go, we said. My people were from South Texas. I've never been across the border."

"I know."

"What is it, Dulce? Why have you come?"

"I want to tell you goodbye. I don't think I'll ever get up here again. I can't afford to run back and forth."

"Many people do," her mother said. Dulce knew she meant: migrants. Mexicans.

"I want to know about Papa, about when he left."

Her mother smoothed her trousers across her thighs. "You know. He went to see his mother. He didn't come back."

"Why? Was he so terrible, to do that? I never understood."

"Why do you want to know now?" Her mother waved her arm, gesturing around the room. "I have made a very good life here. I made a good life for you.

Just because you chose to leave it—that's not my fault. We would have sent you to college. To business school. Whatever you wanted."

"I did what I wanted. That's not what I came to talk about."

"Salvador belonged in Mexico," her mother said. "He was a country man, a simple man."

"That was so bad?"

"It wasn't bad, Dulce. But it wasn't helpful. It wasn't going to make us any kind of life."

"But you married him!"

"We had dances. It was just a little town. I knew all the boys already. They whistled and made eyes at me. They said things when I walked by. I could ignore the Anglo boys. But the Mexican boys, I minded them. Salvador was working the fields. He came to one of the dances. He was polite. He was soft-spoken. I felt like a queen."

"But he was poor. You knew that from the beginning."

"I was poor! We were all poor! I didn't have any world knowledge. Kids now, even poor kids, they grow up on TV. My parents were like old-country people. No one had TVs then. I didn't know I could get an education and make a better life. Have things."

"Have things," Dulce repeated.

"Yes, *have things*," her mother said.

"And not with my father."

Her mother twisted her wedding band on her finger. "I grew up, married to him. I looked around. I didn't want us to spend our lives in trucks and camps and ratty houses. He never really learned to speak English, you know. He could get by, but he didn't have any feel for it."

"And he went to Mexico."

Her mother looked away. She put her hands together, as in prayer. "He went to see his mother. She was ill, maybe dying." She looked back at Dulce. "And while he was gone, I moved us. I simply—moved."

"I don't understand."

"Yes you do. I thought you always did. Perhaps he wrote, and the letters went back. He called, and the phone was disconnected. Perhaps he came back, though I doubt it. I freed him. I freed myself. We were too different. We were old and new cultures. I wanted to be American."

"I wanted to have a father."

"My husband was a father to you."

"He was a step-father."

"He tried."

"Oh Mother."

Her mother stood. "I have to eat something and go to the hospital. I don't understand, Dulce. I don't see why you would want to bring all this up. What I did—it wasn't an easy thing for me. It was very hard for a long time. But I made a better life. You had a chance."

"But then there was Gustavo."

"Yes."

They were no more than a yard apart. Neither moved toward the other. Dulce felt herself trembling inside, invisibly.

The phone rang. Karen called from somewhere to say it was for her mother.

Her mother gave Dulce a helpless, so-sorry look.

"My friend is waiting," Dulce said. Her mother took a few steps toward the door, behind her.

"Mother!" Karen called.

"I've got it in the kitchen!" her mother called back.

Dulce let herself out. The sun struck her face, hot and bright and clean. As she walked down the curved steps to Maggie's car, she saw her son's white shirt, brilliant in the light. She saw his glossy black hair. She hurried to join him.

* * *

I-10 across the Southwest just about killed us. It was so hot, we filled milk jugs with water to keep in the car. Ahead of us, in the truck, Mo let the boys pour water over their heads. We stopped at markets and bought six packs of pop for them.

We stopped in El Paso for the night. The boys had seen sights and were agitating for sights to see. They wanted to go to Carlsbad Caverns. They wanted to cross into Ciudad Juarez. They wanted to go up to the White Sands Monument. Mo cornered me in a McDonald's, before we found a motel, and asked me what I thought. Standing in the hall by the restrooms, he put his hand on my arm. For a moment, I couldn't speak. I felt so tired and confused, and excited, at the same time, and his hand on my arm was hot. I looked at him and felt perspiration trickling down my breasts under my shirt.

I said Dulce and Gus ought to get to San Marcos, and I was tired, and we didn't have much money. I said it was too hot. I reminded him we had stopped to see the saguaro trees outside Tucson, and then that night he'd found a carnival and taken the boys on lots of rides.

He moved closer to me, so that I could feel his hot breath and smell the sweat staining his shirt under his arms and across his chest. He said, shouldn't we ask Dulce?

So what we did, then, was find a nice motel with a big swimming pool (thanks to Polly's credit card), and then we traipsed across the border into Juarez and found a nice restaurant and ate and ate until I was so full and sleepy I had to prop my head up on my arms. Mo promised the boys he'd take them to Carlsbad before the summer was over. Gus said, probably my dad will want to go. Stevie began fussing, and then cried with a full throat. Her bottom was fiery with heat-rash, and she was the most tired of all.

The boys swam late while Mo watched them. The three of them shared a room. I bathed Stevie and lay with her on one bed while Dulce bathed and washed her long black hair. I turned the TV on low. Gorillas in the Mist *was playing. I had seen it before, but I found myself mesmerized, again, by the idea that a woman would isolate herself like that, up in the mountains of a faraway country, for a bunch of gorillas.*

I fell asleep before Dulce was out of the bathroom.

I woke up crying. She heard me. Maggie, she said, are you okay?

I couldn't stop crying. I sat up and folded over, my head in my arms, and sobbed. I was afraid I would wake Stevie, but I couldn't make myself stop.

She said, why don't you come over here, and talk to me?

It must have been a dream, she said. Don't you remember? Dreams only make you cry when you push them down inside too far.

I was calm again. In the dark, with the light from the grounds seeping through the curtains where I hadn't quite pulled them shut, the room, done in rose and gray, was a soft dark neutral color. The air conditioner hummed. I took my pillow and propped myself up in her bed. She took my hand.

I stayed in a motel like this once, I said. A nice one. As soon as I said it, I knew what I had been dreaming.

Tell me, she said.

Someone my mother was seeing took us to Reno. I was nine, almost ten years old. I remember my mother saying the motel was too expensive, he shouldn't have, that sort of thing. He said motels were cheap in Reno.

I don't remember anything at all about him, not if he was tall or short, or dark or blond. I remember he had a gruff voice, but he was nice to me. He bought candy bars for the car, and he kept asking me, did I need to stop? In the front seats, he and my mother talked in low voices, and, once we had crossed over into California from Oregon—it seemed the most spectacular vista in the world to me—I dozed much of the way into Nevada. The motel was sprawling and glitzy, with lots of lights. He took a room with a sitting room, where they brought in a cot for me. He said I could order room service and watch TV, and they would be back.

My mother called me once that night, to ask if I was all right, and I said I was. I didn't go to sleep until two in the morning.

When I woke, they hadn't come home. I waited, with the TV on loud, and at noon I ordered a cheeseburger and a Coke and fries and asked them to bring it all to my room.

The whole day passed. I never left the motel room. I ordered food again in the evening, and turned up the volume on the TV. By then I had begun to cry, sporadically, like a spring rain.

The second morning, the office called to ask if we were checking out. I couldn't say anything at all; my throat constricted so tightly it ached. Shortly, someone from the office came to the room and knocked. I called out Who is it! *the way my mother had taught me, and I wouldn't open the door.*

That afternoon a lady came. She said she was from child welfare. She asked me a lot of questions, but I didn't know the answers. I didn't know why my mother and the man had left me in the motel, or where they had gone, or if they were coming back. I wondered what this woman would do to me.

That night I stayed in a house in Reno. It was a family house, with a mother and a father and a girl a little older than me. They were very nice to me. We went out for pizza.

In a few days another lady came and got me, and drove me back to Oregon, to my aunt's house. Then someone from child welfare there came to talk to me, and I still didn't know anything. I thought my mother was dead, but I didn't cry.

My aunt had a baby, and her husband, who worked in the woods, had no work just then. He was always in the house, and he didn't like having me there, but when they had a fight about it—I could hear everything through the wall—she reminded him that they were getting money for me. I tried to help. I picked up any little thing that fell to the floor. I played with the baby. I tried to do the dishes. I knew I wouldn't get to stay; I was waiting for someone to come again, from child welfare, and move me to a new place. I wanted to call and ask when she would come, but I didn't know how to call. One night, while my aunt was bathing the baby, her husband sat by me on the sofa to watch TV. He moved close. He put his hand on my leg. He was drinking beer. He leaned down and whispered in my ear.

He said, you're just a little twig off your mama's tree, ain't you. My face was burning, and my ears were ringing, and I made myself think about the mountains I had seen on the way to Reno.

In time, someone did come and take me to a new family's house. When my mother returned, she came to see me there. She said she wanted me to come home with her, but they wouldn't let me. She said it would take a while. She didn't tell me where she had been.

She had cut her hair and bleached it, but she was still my mother. She had gained weight, too. Her breasts strained against her old blouse, and her jeans were tight. She called me Dolly and Angel and said I'd come home soon. She had found a new job, in a Mexican restaurant. She was sorry, she finally said. She thought he would work out for us, but he didn't. She never told me where she'd gone.

I was waiting for Dulce to ask where my father was. I had been asked that so many times, growing up. I didn't know. I guess my mother didn't know. Welfare wanted to find him. It terrified me, I thought they would send me off to him somewhere, a stranger, but now I know they wanted to find him and make him pay something for my care. They didn't have anything to go on, though. He never had to pay.

Dulce said, You're a good mother, that's what matters now. She said this fiercely, a way I'd never heard her speak.

Then she asked: What happened to your mother after that? Did she leave again?

I couldn't speak. She turned toward me, and held her arms so I could slide into her embrace.

I thought about the people who had ever held me close. My mother, too long ago to remember. Polly, the way a mother does. Gretchen, her leg lying dead weight over mine, her arm flung across my waist. Mo.

Then I slept. We all slept late, even Stevie. It was good we did. I wasn't prepared for west Texas. The vastness, the emptiness, terrified me. I couldn't imagine we would ever come out on the other side.

January 1977

* * *

Maggie's mother, Angela, lived in the same town she'd grown up in. She'd gone away once, to Portland, but she hated the city more than she hated the boredom back home. Another time, she lived for a year in Eugene. She came back pregnant. Her own mother had moved on years before, first to Washington, then to somewhere in Utah.

When she was a little girl, she used to go in the good weather down to the river and play on the rocks. You had to cross the bridge to reach the town. In early summer, when the water was still high, boys jumped off the bridge. It was low enough they could cannonball and swim ten yards and be in shallow water. Their legs would be bright red from the impact. The girls would watch, and giggle.

It had been raining for a week, and then the temperature fell suddenly, overnight. In the morning, all over the county, cars skidded on black ice. A school bus went off the road, but nobody was hurt.

Maggie wanted to know what her mother did that day, but there was no one to ask. Maybe she slept late, then watched soaps, had a little something to eat. She called Maggie after school, but she had nothing special to say. Maggie tried so hard to remember, but she couldn't. They were stiff with one another; their lives were separate. Maggie was living with a high school teacher's family. She was studying, getting good grades; she was learning to sew.

The little town was very dark at night. There was only a sliver of moon, and even that was obscured by clouds. While Maggie slept, her mother Angela walked down to the bridge, dressed in jeans, a heavy pullover sweater, and short boots.

It was so dark, when she leaned over the bridge, she probably didn't see the water at all. She didn't leap into the river; she leaped into the night.

Maybe she fell. She heard something; she had had a few beers. She leaned over, she wondered what the sound was, the bridge was slippery, she fell.

* * *

At last, we drove into green and hilly country. We'd thought we would reach San Marcos for dinner, but the boys were too hungry to wait. We stopped to eat tacos. Dulce called ahead to let her mother-in-law know how we were doing. She came back to our booth and said that the Quirartes said they had plenty of room; we could all spend the night. Aw, it's not that far going on to Austin, Mo said, but I said I thought we should. The children were worn out; so was I. And I thought it would be better to arrive at Mo's Austin place earlier in the day, so that we would have time to adjust a little, all of us to one another in a new place.

Mo asked Dulce what she thought of the tacos. She said they were good—the pork was roasted, the salsa was fresh—but she still liked them with soft tortillas, the way her mother made them, back when her mother still cooked.

In the car again, she told me she thought he was cute. I had to laugh.

He's little, I said. But I guess he is cute.

She said she liked small men. I know you Anglos like these giants, taking up a lot of space in the world, but I like a more compact man.

And Gustavo? He's cute too?

He's beautiful, she said. I thought about her dream.

Will you be with him? I asked. Will you live with him again? Could you go back to Oregon?

She was wearing her hair in a long braid that hung over her shoulder. She stroked it as she spoke.

I'll stay at his parents' house at first, she said. He's living with his brother's family. I'll help his mother with the house, I'll see what I can learn to do there. There's a college in San Marcos. I'd like to think about that. I'd have to find out if I'm smart enough, if it's not too late. I think Gus needs this, though. In Oregon, there's just me.

But Gustavo, I insisted. You love him, don't you?

I have to take care of Gus, and take care of myself, and then I'll see about loving him. I have to think about how we'll live.

It might be easier the other way around, I said. Loving, and then finding a way. I knew I was talking to myself; I'd read enough novels to figure out the way a line of dialogue like that works. I know characters tell other people the things they themselves need to hear. Or novelists make them speak feelings they have, or wish for.

I haven't seen him in five years, she said. The last time I saw him he was behind a glass panel in a gray room, and he told me I should make my own life. He didn't know if he would make it. He had nothing for me. I went back to the house where I was staying—I had been staying with a cousin of his from Texas, she begged me to go to his parents' but I wanted my mother—and I packed and took a bus to Oregon. I haven't thought I would live with him since then.

But you dream about him. I had to say it.

She finally smiled. If he is wearing a bandana, I won't be able to resist. If he has his hair long, like the first time I saw him. If he's proud of Gus, of what I've done.

So there's hope, I said. She let that stand. She probably knew who I was talking to.

I wanted to ask her about Gustavo's mother, but I remem-

bered that she had never met her. I wondered if she would like me.

I thought Jay would like to see the animals on the farm. And cheese in a wheel. We wouldn't have to hurry, leaving.

The Quirarte farm came into view as we pulled over a hill and rode toward a deep blue sky. It's really pretty, I said.

I was thinking about the dream you had about me, I told her. I was thinking while we were driving, and I could see it: me at the window of a house, looking out over the yard. I think—I think that down there, in the yard, there would be people I know, Polly and my friends, and Mo, and the kids, of course, but other people, too, like the Safeway checker and the pharmacist. And you.

A daydream, she said.

We had pulled up into the yard near the house, and dogs were barking and people were running out to greet us. I reached over and squeezed her hand. I wanted to wish her well; I wanted to make everything work out, but all I could do was wish for myself the very thing she'd dreamed.

I'll tell you something, I said before we got out of the car. I'm sure I was happy. In the dream. I don't know why, exactly, but I think I'll know, sooner or later. All of it could be true. I could be happy.

Contemporary Fiction for Your Enjoyment

☐ **ANNIE JOHN by Jamaica Kincaid.** The island of Antigua is a magical place; growing up there should be a sojourn in paradise for young Annie John. But as in the basket of green figs carried on her mother's head, there is a snake hidden somewhere within. "Penetrating, relentless . . . Women especially will learn much about their childhood through this eloquent, profound story." —*San Francisco Chronicle* (263565—$8.95)

☐ **MIDDLE PASSAGE by Charles Johnson.** "A story of slavery . . . a tale of travel and tragedy, yearning and history . . . brilliant, riveting."—*San Francisco Chronicle* (266386—$10.00)

☐ **COPPER CROWN by Lane von Herzen.** The story of two young women—one white, one black—sharing a friendship amidst the divisive and violent racism of rural 1913 Texas. "A fresh, poetically evocative and down-to-earth novel."—*The Washington Post* (269164—$10.00)

☐ **BEYOND DESERVING by Sandra Scofield.** Filled with telling, poignant details of family conflict and the redeeming power of love, this vividly imagined work announces the arrival of an important new voice in American fiction. "Wise and engaging . . . a tightly drawn portrait of a fascinating family."—Chicago Tribune (269075—$10.00)

☐ **WALKING DUNES by Sandra Scofield.** A powerful and atmospheric glimpse into small-town life at a time when the world was shifting as fast as the white sands of the Texas plains. "Remarkable for its insight and power . . . finely etched and sensitive . . . an impressive read."—*Publishers Weekly* (270278—$10.00)

Prices slightly higher in Canada.

Visa and Mastercard holders can order Plume, Meridian, and Dutton books by calling **1-800-253-6476**.

They are also available at your local bookstore. Allow 4-6 weeks for delivery. This offer is subject to change without notice.